BACHE

Student Nurse Pippa Benedict's sister
married a consultant, so Pippa has a
reputation to live up to at St Clem's.
But after her first disastrous day on Men's
Surgical, she knows for sure that there's
one consultant she won't be marrying—
and that's blue-eyed cardiologist, Julius
Sterling!

BACHELOR OF HEARTS

BY

LEONIE CRAIG

MILLS & BOON LIMITED
15–16 BROOK'S MEWS
LONDON W1A 1DR

First published in Great Britain 1985
by Mills & Boon Limited

© Leonie Craig 1985

Australian copyright 1985
Philippine copyright 1985

ISBN 0 263 75081 7

Set in 11 on 11½ pt Linotron Times
03–0685–46,900

Photoset by Rowland Phototypesetting Ltd
Bury St Edmunds, Suffolk
Made and printed in Great Britain by
Richard Clay (The Chaucer Press) Ltd
Bungay, Suffolk

For Eifion, who provides the facts,
and for Wendy, who helped put them
together.

CHAPTER ONE

'RIGHT.' Sister Tutor's voice gathered the immediate, rapt attention of twenty pairs of eyes. 'Gather round. We still have a lot to get through. I intend to begin by shattering a few illusions, and reminding you of the first basic principles of nursing, for those of you who might still be in doubt.'

There was a loud, communal groan. 'Have a heart, Sister.'

Sister beamed benignly. 'I am *all* heart, Male Nurse Patterson, which is why you have survived your first eleven weeks at this training school. But if any of you have the idea that nursing is going to be fun, fun, fun, let me put the record straight at the outset. For the next three years "work" is the only word which need hold any significance for you. Work, work and still more work.'

Pippa Benedict ducked her head to whisper, 'It looks like we're going to have to work, folks.'

Sister's eye honed in unerringly on the culprit. 'Thank you, Nurse Benedict. I'm delighted to see you understand. And now,' she turned her attention to the group, 'if we can get on. Nurse Patterson, put Gertrude away in the cupboard please.' There were giggles as Rick Patterson grasped the life-sized dummy in a passionate embrace. 'Thank you, Nurse. Quietly and quickly please. We are not here to be entertained. Sit down all of you.'

The group obeyed, eyes fixed on the navy-clad figure. 'Now, you have all been given details of your new set. Half of you will go to medical, half to surgical wards. If you haven't got the name of your particular ward, see me afterwards. In all cases, however, the rules are the same. You will be seen only if necessary and heard not at all, unless addressed directly.'

'The original three monkeys,' Sylvia Fox muttered. 'See no evil . . .'

'In your case, Nurse Fox, you may well be advised to practise all three.' Sister paused significantly. 'I shall of course be receiving reports on each of you, so be warned.'

There was a general groan and Sister smiled. 'I don't anticipate that any of you will let me down. I certainly wouldn't advise it.'

Her gaze lingered for a moment on Pippa Benedict's lowered head, then moved to the notes she held. 'For those of you going to surgical wards, an extra word of warning. You will be *observing*. Should you have any doubts, *ask*, don't guess. Anything you will be asked to do you will have covered here in class, so you simply need to remember what you've been taught. During consultants' rounds you will merge into the background. Keep your hands behind your backs and remain silent.'

'Damn, and there was I hoping to pick up a dashing number in a white coat.' Jane Greaves sighed heavily and Sister eyed her with tolerant amusement.

'I hate to disappoint you, Nurse, but let me assure you that consultants do not recognise the lower forms of life, of which you are one.' She beamed innocently, ignoring another mutter of protest. 'Oh, it has happened that one of our nurses has married a consultant.' A loud cheer punctuated the lecture and Sister's gaze came to rest briefly on one particular flushed face.

Pippa cringed as low as possible in the hard plastic chair, and battled with a sigh. It was bad enough having to live up to the reputation of having a sister who had also worked at St Clement's. Even worse to have to live *down* the fact that she had married the most eligible senior consultant on its staff.

'But it is so rare an occurrence,' Sister went on, 'that you can all safely dismiss it from your schedules.' The notes were consulted again. 'Another point for those of you going to Surgical. Should Sister be occupied, you will report to Staff Nurse. This applies in particular to those of you allotted to Pasteur Ward, where the new consultant cardiologist will be taking his first round, probably some time today. This means that Sister Carson will probably be involved in doing a detailed round of patients in order that he can get to know them and their histories in detail, and makes it even more important that you should not get in the way. Is that clearly understood?'

They nodded and chanted, 'Yes, Sister.'

'Good. I'm sure Staff Nurse will find work to keep you all fully occupied. And now perhaps we can go on to this morning's lecture which is, if you read your notes as instructed, and I trust you did . . .' there was a general shuffling and murmur of assent '. . . the sterile procedure for changing and dressing a post-operative wound. So, if we can have a patient please. Nurse Jones?'

'But I was the blanket bath, Sister.'

'Well how nice for you.' Sister reached for an enveloping white gown, mask and gloves. 'And now you are going to be a post-operative wound. It must be your lucky day. Hop on to the couch. The rest of you gather round. Not too closely.' She flapped them away and reached for the trolley.

Pippa Benedict stared lethargically out of the window, stifling a yawn. There was something almost hypnotic about the sun streaming warmly through the windows on to her arms in the short-sleeved dress, and the buzzing of the bees, darting lazily around the bushes, their droning mingling with Sister's voice in the background.

She watched sleepily, her gaze following a chattering group of third-year nurses as they emerged through the swing doors of the main block to cross to the nurses' home, and she felt a pang of envy. Was it really possible that some day she would look like that, wear the uniform with its neat red belt with such assurance? Her fingers went instinctively to the ridiculous white cap which somehow never sat quite so correctly on her own mass of auburn hair, no matter how many extra pins she used to try to keep it in place.

She sighed and caught the heady waft of roses from beneath the window, and felt her nose tingle with a brief but tantalising pang of homesickness. Wiltshire was a far cry from Dover. It was funny that she hadn't realised how much she would miss the sea, early morning walks along the front, watching the ferries coming in and out, the car-loads full of holiday-makers, faces full of anticipation.

She sighed again, unaware that the sound carried, remembering the unbelievable wrench of leaving home for the first time. Still, she had made a lot of good friends and they had already spent some happy times exploring the nearby, fascinating old city of Salisbury with its huge cathedral, the dozens of little bookshops tucked away in odd corners and the river winding its way attractively through the town. Her lips twitched into a smile. Yes, there was a great deal to be said for independence.

'Are we keeping you from something more important, Nurse Benedict? If so, please feel free to leave and return when you can give us more of your time and attention.'

Pippa turned to regard Sister with a smile. 'Oh no, that's quite all right, thank you, S . . .'

Muffled giggles brought her back to reality with a jerk and she stared at Sister Tutor's frosty gaze. 'That is . . . no, Sister. Sorry, Sister.'

'I'm pleased to hear it, Nurse. I dislike waste, and time is one of the most precious commodities you have if any of you are to complete your training and emerge at the end of it with the qualifications I must assume you came here to gain.'

The look of pained disapproval was Sister's greatest weapon, and she knew how to use it to advantage. Pippa stared abjectly at her feet. 'Yes, Sister.'

'Dare I hope that you have absorbed anything of this lecture, Nurse?'

'Oh yes, Sister.' Dark eyes widened confidently.

'Good, I'm pleased to hear it. Then perhaps you would care to continue. I was about to demonstrate the procedure for applying a dressing to a post-operative wound which is discharging. Will you be good enough to pass the swabs for cleansing the area?'

Pippa stared blankly at the trolley, seeing a maze of packs and gleaming instruments. Conscious of twenty pairs of eyes and a rising panic, she reached out blindly for the nearest pack to hand and thrust it toward Sister's outstretched hand.

A look of horror transfixed Sister's face. 'I'm sterile, you idiot girl. Don't you know what that means?'

Pippa felt the tears of mortification welling up as she gulped. 'Y . . . yes. I mean . . . no, Sister.'

'Obviously not.' The mask was lowered, rubber gloves snapped off and the 'patient' ordered smartly back into line. 'I see little point in continuing this lecture. Clearly some of you find this aspect of your training both boring and unnecessary. A point upon which I shall clearly have to re-educate you, tomorrow morning.'

An audible gasp met the words. 'But Sister, that's our morning off, for study.'

'It *was* your morning off. Unfortunately I have a schedule to keep and any disruptions, as you will quickly come to learn, will be made up for in your time, not mine. Therefore I would suggest, Nurses, that you do your studying tonight instead—because I shall require a ten-page essay from each of you by the end of the week on sterile procedures. Nurse Benedict, you will make that twenty pages, since you obviously know so much more about the subject already that you don't feel the need to add to that knowledge. And now, I would suggest that you go for your tea-break and then report to the various wards allotted to you this morning. You will of course make yourselves known to the senior member of staff on duty.' The grey head nodded dismissal and the group began to disperse, flinging mutinous looks in Pippa's direction.

Outside she stopped in her tracks, dropped her

shoulder bag on to the grass and followed it with a sigh of relief as she sat back and turned her face up to the sun. 'I suppose that means I've earned myself a black mark.'

'I should think if you make that twenty you'll be nearer the mark.' Liz Dixon shook her head, watching Sister's retreating back. 'Honestly, Benedict, you really are a prize idiot. You know how important this lecture was. We've got a written exam coming up in two weeks' time as well as the essay you've landed us with. I heard definite mutterings of revenge.'

They watched the rest of the group drift towards main block, unhappily trailing books and bags. 'I know. You don't need to rub it in.'

'Well you'll never get through at this rate. Come to think of it, neither will I.' Liz tugged at a daisy and tossed it thoughtlessly aside. 'Frankly, I don't know what I'll do if I don't get through.'

Pippa frowned and chewed on a piece of grass. 'I'm sorry, honestly. Trouble is, I had a letter from Emma. She's living in Cornwall, lucky devil, and it made me think how nice it would be to be on a beach somewhere instead of that stuffy old lecture room.'

'Yes, well you'll have all the time in the world for beaches if you don't pull your socks up. You know while we're in PTS we're still more or less on trial and everything depends on our results as to whether or not we're allowed to stay on.'

'I know. I know. I only let my attention wander for a minute.'

'Long enough to have missed the entire point of the lecture.'

Pippa grinned. 'I thought I'd die when Sister

suddenly screamed "I'm sterile, you idiot, sterile!"
For a second I thought she was talking about some
personal gynae problem.'

Liz shook her head. 'I really don't know what
we're going to do with you. Why can't you just
learn to fold your hands meekly, say, "Yes, Sister,
no, Sister"?'

'Three bags full, Sister.' She grimaced. 'Sorry.
Lord, I could do with that cup of tea. We'd better
make a move.'

Liz looked at her watch and leapt to her feet with
a yelp, hitching her bag to her shoulder. 'Oh no. I
don't believe it! We'd better make a move all right,
because we're due on the ward in three minutes
flat.'

'But we can't be.' Pippa screeched with horror,
dropped her books and had to go back for them.
She bundled them frantically into her bag and ran.
'We're not going to make it. I know we're not!'

'Well we'd better start hoping we do. Come on.'

'I've got the stitch.'

'Never mind the stitch. It's nothing compared to
what we'll get if we don't make it.' Liz's face was
red with exertion as she ran, and she found herself
suddenly jerked to a halt as Pippa caught hold of
her arm. 'What are you doing, for heaven's sake?'

'This way. We can go this way, it's quicker.'

Liz slowed and followed her gaze in horror.
'You're joking. You know we're not allowed to go
through the private wing.'

'Well who's going to know?' Pippa sagged,
breathing hard, trying to relieve the pain in her
side. 'We can cut across the lawns, out through the
side gate and into the back entrance of the main
block.'

'And have you any idea of what will happen if we get caught?'

'I jolly well know what will happen if we're late. Sister made it pretty clear that I'm at the head of her list of candidates most likely to fail, and if I get a bad report now, I'm out.' Pippa straightened up. 'I'm going to risk it, anyway. You chance the other way if you like. After all, I'm the one in trouble and you don't stand to get your future prospects lopped off even if you are late just this once. You can always make some excuse.'

'You don't seriously imagine for one minute it would be accepted, do you?' Liz muttered dryly. 'Anyway, I'll stick with you, though God knows why.'

'You're a pal.'

'I'm an idiot.'

'Well let's go.' Pippa hoisted her bag on to her shoulder and eyed the block which housed the private wing as they ran across the grass. 'Let's just hope some beady-eyed sister isn't keeping look-out.'

Their feet flew across the neatly cropped grass as the private wing slumbered in a gathering haze of summer heat. Nurses weren't allowed to sit and study in this area. It was reserved strictly, and very unfairly, Pippa thought, for visiting doctors and relatives and those patients who wished to take the air. 'I just hope none of them choose now,' she muttered to herself under her breath. 'Come on Through that gate and we're safe.'

'I'm right with you,' called Liz.

A violent thud almost knocked the breath out of her body as she collided with Pippa's retreating figure and they both sprawled on the grass.

'What on earth are you doing?'

'Quiet. Over there.'

Cowering behind the hedge, they watched as two sisters and a staff nurse emerged from the block and sauntered, chatting, along the path ahead of them towards the nurses' home.

'Oh no. That's all we need. Look, we can still make it, with a bit of luck,' Liz urged. 'If we run fast enough they probably won't notice, and even if they do they won't recognise us.'

'They may not notice you,' Pippa breathed. 'But how far do you think I'd get with my colour hair?'

Liz fell back and groaned. 'Oh lor, then there's only one thing for it. We can hop over the hedge. It's not very high. Come on.' She was away and Pippa lurched to her feet, clutching at her cap and dragging her bag behind her.

She eyed the hedge. Liz was right, it wasn't that high. Thank heaven for sensible shoes, she thought, as she dug a foot firmly on to the lower rail of the fence and jumped. Easy. Down the grass bank, across the road and into main block.

Except that she couldn't move. 'Liz,' she hissed frantically. 'Liz, I'm stuck.' She twisted round to stare with horror at her skirt, which was hooked up in the branches. She dropped her bag and began wrenching furiously at the hem. 'Oh no, I don't believe it. Not now. You can't do this to me. Liz . . .'

'Perhaps I can be of some help?' a voice said calmly, and she spun round, hot with fury and humiliation, to stare into the face of a very tall man whose grey and ridiculously long-lashed eyes regarded her with mild curiosity.

She gulped hard, suddenly all too conscious of the large expanse of long, black-stockinged leg she was revealing, and tugged even more furiously at her skirt, feeling the tightening of her throat and her eyes blurring with tears of acute embarrassment. Where was Liz?

'I'm afraid your friend was last seen disappearing at a rate of knots across the lawn.' She was sure there was a gleam of laughter in his eyes as he said it, and, to her dismay, he began quite coolly to disentangle her dress from the hedge.

'I can manage,' she hissed, as the long, slim hands made unwitting contact with her skin so that she blushed even harder.

'For heaven's sake don't struggle like that. You're making things worse. Just stand perfectly still and I'll have you free in seconds.'

It was easier said than done, she thought, as she closed her eyes and opened them again to stare at his lowered head and the thick, dark hair curling against his collar. She squirmed with even greater determination. 'Oh, please do hurry.'

He straightened up and she felt herself released. She tugged her skirt down quickly over the gaping hole in her stocking, defying him to laugh.

He didn't. 'Should you be here anyway?' He looked around him and Pippa gained an even stronger impression of his height, which must be quite six feet, she thought. Good-looking too, though not so young, she added, grudgingly. At least thirty-five. He turned to look at her. 'Surely this isn't the usual route to . . . wherever it is you're going?'

'No, of course it isn't. This is the private wing and you're not supposed to be here either.' She stopped as his eyebrows rose mildly. 'Well, I suppose it's different if you're visiting a patient.' Her gaze went beyond him to the sleek black car and she felt a faint quiver of envy. It was the kind of car a man like that *would* drive, of course. 'Well in that case . . .' She swallowed hard and studied the bank of grass sloping down to the road.

His hand suddenly clasped hers in a strong firm grip which did very strange things to her heartbeat. 'Allow me to help, before you have any more accidents.'

She stood on the road, freed her hand quickly and thrust it behind her back, trying to ignore the tingling sensation which seemed to be running through it.

'Actually,' she offered by way of explanation, though not sure why it should be necessary, 'I'm supposed to be on Pasteur Ward but I got held up and Sister Carson will kill me if I'm late.'

'That sounds a little unreasonable. Can't you simply explain?'

She treated him to a look of disdain. How could anyone be so naive? 'Sisters don't listen to excuses. That's why I was taking the short cut, not that it's made any difference. It looks as if I shall be late anyway now.' She peered glumly at her uniform. 'Besides, Sister is bound to be all of a twitter because of the new consultant who's arriving today.'

Grey eyes considered her solemnly. 'And why should that make her . . . all of a twitter?'

'Well, I've no idea.' She shrugged. 'Consultants are only human beings after all, aren't they?' She thought about it for a second. 'Well, perhaps this one has two heads or something. Personally, I can't

see what all the fuss is about, for one man. He's
probably in his dotage anyway.'

'I expect you're right.' He joined her in a quick
laugh of mutual sympathy, then looked at his
watch. 'Hadn't you better get going? You might
still just make it. You never know, Sister might be
kept too busy with this new man to notice if you slip
in quietly.'

'Oh lor, yes.' She turned, then stopped. 'Thanks
a million. I might have been stuck there for ever.'

'I doubt that.' His smile was nice. 'I'm quite sure
someone would have come to the rescue.'

She let that pass. 'By the way, if you want private
reception, it's just around the corner. You can't
miss it. You can park your car in front.'

He waved an acknowledgement and was already
striding towards the car as she turned to fling one
last, curious glance in his direction. Yes, he wasn't
at all bad-looking, she thought. In fact very nice.
Whoever he was visiting didn't know how lucky she
was. Or perhaps she did, came the unrewarding
thought, which refused to go away and left a depressing cloud hovering over her for the rest of the
afternoon.

CHAPTER TWO

Liz was waiting for her, and she rushed through the swing doors on Men's Surgical to find herself being steered relentlessly towards the kitchen. A tray of plastic jugs was thrust into her hands and Liz nodded in the direction of an apron.

'Quick, make yourself useful. Start filling those.' She flung a harassed look over her shoulder. 'For heaven's sake, where did you get to? I've been going frantic.'

Pippa stared at the jugs, breathing hard and feeling her cheeks redden. 'I got caught up.'

'Caught up? Well honestly, I felt a right idiot chattering away to myself, I can tell you.'

'Oh lor, sorry.' She carried the tray to the sink, winding the apron round her waist. 'Hadn't I better report to Sister or something?'

'You can't. She's incarcerated in the office.'

'Oh, nasty. Well Staff then?'

'She's in there too, and not in the best of tempers I may say, which is why we're in here trying at least to look as if we're busy.'

'Damn, I suppose that means I'm already down in the little black book.'

'I don't think whatever the emergency is has anything to do with you; not this time anyway,' Liz offered reassurance. 'Not that I know how you manage it. You must have the luck of the devil. Anyway, you can stop panicking. I told Staff you were hot on my heels but that a visitor had stopped you to ask for directions and you were being an angel of mercy. I don't know that she was convinced, but it was the best I could think of and she didn't do anything, apart from mutter.'

'Bless you, and you'll never know how close to the truth it was, except that I wasn't the one being the angel of mercy.'

'What on earth are you talking about?' Liz peered into the cupboards. 'Now where do you suppose they hide the orange? Ah, here. Top those jugs up with cordial, will you?'

Pippa took the bottle, tipped a generous measure in and eyed it doubtfully. 'Well, I was right behind you, but my skirt got caught in the hedge and I'd still be there now if some man hadn't come along and unhooked me. It was very embarrassing.'

Liz stared at her. 'You're joking! No, you're not joking. Honestly, how do you do it?'

'What, get caught up on hedges?'

'No, idiot. Get rescued by strange men. I take it he was dishy, too?'

Pippa concentrated defensively on the orange juice. 'I've no idea. All I could think about was the gaping hole in my stockings.' She caught Liz's eye. 'Well, yes I suppose he was rather, in a distant, cool sort of way.'

'Not exactly distant from the sound of things. So who was he?'

'How should I know? I mean it's hardly the sort of thing you get round to at a time like that. Anyway, we're not likely to come across him over here. He was obviously visiting someone in the private wing.'

'Typical,' Liz snorted. 'Not that it probably isn't

just as well. The last thing we need right now is any kind of diversion with the present flap on. You'd think royalty was visiting instead of the new consultant cardiologist. He's doing his first round this afternoon and Staff is running round like a chicken with its head cut off.'

'Well, personally I think all this fuss for one man is unreasonable.'

'For pity's sake don't let Staff hear you say that. As far as she's concerned, anything in a dark suit ranks among the gods. Of course, there are the greater and lesser varieties, but from the way she's twitching I'd say this one definitely ranks among the greater.'

'I wonder if we should curtsy?' Pippa was smiling as the door opened and Staff Nurse Baker's figure filled the doorway.

'What are you nurses doing in here? Surely you can find something more useful to do?' Her gaze flickered crossly to Pippa. 'And who exactly are you?'

'Er, Nurse Benedict, Staff. I'm from PTS.'

'You didn't report to me.'

'No, Staff. I've only just come on to the ward.'

An expression of distaste cut across the stout features. 'Why on earth they have to inflict their students on us I'll never know. I don't see why they couldn't let you practise on another ward where you could do less harm.'

It occurred to Pippa that by Staff Nurse Baker's logic no nurse would ever learn anything, but she caught Liz's warning glance and compressed her lips meekly. 'Yes, Staff.'

'In future just remember that I wish to be informed when anyone comes on to this ward.'

'Actually, Staff,' Liz said, 'I did explain to Sister.'

'I'm quite sure Nurse Benedict can speak for herself, thank you, Nurse.' The voice was tinged with irritation. 'In any case, I've neither the time nor inclination to discuss it now. In future just bear in mind that rules are rules and not made to be flouted, particularly by students who are still wet behind the ears.' She clucked, resentfully. 'I don't know what it is about girls these days, but they seem to have very strange ideas about what nursing is. Well let me tell you, I can spot a trouble-maker a mile off and I won't have any on my ward. Is that perfectly clear?'

Pippa laced her fingers tightly together behind her back and muttered, meekly, 'Yes, Staff.'

'What are you doing here, anyway?'

'Filling the water jugs, Staff.'

'Yes, well it doesn't take two of you to perform a simple task like that, and you needn't get the idea that the pair of you are going to be allowed to stick together, huddling in corners for girlish chats. This is a busy ward. Nurse Benedict, come with me. I want several of the beds stripped and re-made. You can give Nurse Gibson a hand and be quick about it. Mr Sterling will be here at two-fifteen to do his round, and I want you safely out of sight before then.'

Casting a glance of sympathy in Liz's direction, Pippa scuttled dutifully after Staff Nurse Baker's retreating figure as she made her way along the ward which was, at the moment, relatively quiet. The lunch-time trolley was long gone, leaving behind lingering memories of fish, which obviously met with as stern a disapproval as did student nurses. 'We'll have some windows open in here, Nurse.'

A second-year in pink gingham leapt to obey, managing to send a twinkling glance in Pippa's direction as she did so. It was heartening, offering the first hint that perhaps Men's Surgical wasn't going to be quite as bad as she had imagined.

The hope faded as she hopped to an abrupt halt, narrowly avoiding stepping on Staff Nurse Baker's heels. 'Nurse Gibson, I want the two end beds stripped and re-made. Both patients are due for discharge. Ring Reception and see what's happened to their transport, will you? I don't like having discharged patients wandering around the ward, getting in everyone's way.'

'I'll do that, Staff.' Pete Gibson's good-natured grin went over Staff Nurse Baker's shoulder to where Pippa offered a shy smile in response and bit her lip, suppressing a giggle, as he winked broadly. She looked away quickly. 'I think Mr Franks is just saying a few goodbyes, Staff, and Mr Sloane is still finishing his packing.'

'Well give him a hand with it please, Nurse, and then ask them both to kindly wait in the day room until their cars arrive. We've another emergency admission due in some time today, and a routine one tomorrow morning, so snap to it. This is Nurse Benedict from PTS, by the way. Show her what to do, will you, and do it quietly. We shall have quite enough disruptions on the ward this afternoon as it is, without students getting underfoot.'

She was gone, leaving Pippa to swallow hard on the lump of resentment which suddenly seemed to be blocking her throat. She wondered whether the next three years were going to be tolerable, let alone worthwhile, if she had to battle against the constantly bigoted attitude of people like Staff Nurse Baker. She blinked the suspicion of a tear away as Pete Gibson squeezed her arm.

'Oh come on, it's not as bad as you think.'

'Isn't it?' She looked up at the tall figure in the white coat which bore the navy epaulettes of a third-year nurse, and the good-looking face above it. 'I have the distinct feeling I've just managed to get off to a bad start, and the ridiculous thing is, I'm not even sure what I've done wrong.'

He laughed. 'Don't take it so personally.'

'But I thought it *was* personal.'

He grinned as he removed a chart from the board at the end of one of the beds and inserted a new one. 'Believe me, you've not been singled out for any special privileges. That's just Baker's way. Admittedly it comes over a little more strongly when she comes face to face with someone as pretty as you.' Pippa blushed beneath the speculative glance. 'It's not jealousy exactly. At least, Baker wouldn't admit to it. But in her opinion nursing is still a vocation which should exclude everything else from our lives.'

'Oh dear.'

'As you say. Still, we all live in the hope that some day Baker's prince will come along and find a heart beating beneath that starched white bodice. Trouble is, with Baker's luck she'll kiss him and he'll turn into a frog.'

A chuckle burst from her lips to be stifled hastily as Sister emerged, frowning, from the office. Pippa bent over the bed to flap a clean sheet towards Pete as the figure approached, tall, slim and neat.

'Try to work quietly please, Nurse. Our patients need their rest.'

'Yes, Sister. Sorry, Sister.'

Lisa Carson paused. 'You're new here, aren't you?'

Pippa felt her heart give a slight lurch. 'Yes, Sister. I came over from PTS today.'

'Well, welcome to Men's Surgical. I hope you'll enjoy your stay with us. Unfortunately you've picked a bad day. We have a new consultant arriving shortly. I'd suggest you find something else to do when you've finished here, where you won't get in the way.'

'Yes, Sister.' Pippa released her breath slowly as she watched her walk away. 'She's nice.'

'Who, Carson? You're right. I'll second that.'

Pippa followed his speculative gaze and thought she caught a gleam in his eye which added to her own feeling that any girl would need to watch herself where Pete Gibson was concerned. Not that she had any time at this stage of her career for that kind of involvement, she reminded herself forcibly. Right now she had her work cut out just surviving PTS and staying on her feet all day.

Biting back a small sigh, she turned her attention to her work, tucking the corners of the sheet into a neat envelope, just as she had been taught in training school. She stood back with a nod of self-satisfaction. 'There, not bad if I do say so myself.'

'Take my word for it, after the first thousand you'll hate the sight of them. Just wait till you've stripped and made every bed on the ward and Staff comes along and makes you do them all over again.'

'She wouldn't?' Her eyes widened, suspecting he might be joking.

'Don't count on it. I've seen more than one student reduced to tears. The thing is to regard it all as part of the toughening process and don't let it get you down. Things do improve.'

'Is that a promise, and if so when exactly? Because I'm already wondering if I'll be able to stay the course.'

'Oh, I'd say round about the fourth year. When you've done your finals and had the results.' He laughed at the look of horror on her face and relented. 'You'll make it, unless of course some man comes along and persuades you to throw it all up in favour of motherhood and slippers by the fire.'

'Isn't that a rather male chauvinist attitude?'

His brows rose. 'And aren't you being a prickly feminist?'

'Not at all,' she retorted crossly. 'I'm all in favour of marriage and . . . motherhood, even slippers by the fire.'

'I'm jolly glad to hear it. All vital, life-supporting factors.'

Pippa chose to ignore the provocative look in his eyes. 'Women do have careers too these days, you know. And I don't intend giving up nursing so easily just because some man beckons.'

'Hey, who's arguing?' He held up his hands in mock submission.

'I thought you were.'

'Not a bit of it. I just like testing the reaction, that's all.'

And I fell for it, she thought, thumping the pillow a little too vigorously as the image of one particular man floated into her mind, surprising her with the thought that slippers by the fire might not be so bad—provided they belonged to the right man, of course. She tilted her head unconsciously on one side. Not that he had looked in the least bit like a slippers by the fire man. And even if he was, someone else would undoubtedly be warming them for him. She moved dejectedly away from the thought to the next bed.

'It's very quiet, isn't it? I expected Men's Surgical to be noisy.'

'Usually it is, but Monday is our big intake day for ops. We do all the routine ones, the patients who were asked to come in the previous day, as well as any emergencies. So we don't have visitors this afternoon as a rule. Hence you may have noticed the mood of glum resignation.'

'I thought that was probably due to the fish at lunch.'

'You noticed.'

She made a face. 'It was hard not to.' Her glance went the length of the attractive twenty-six bed ward, to the figures lying huddled sleepily beneath the blankets. 'I take it they've just come back from Theatre?'

'That's right. And they're all doing nicely. Give them a couple more hours and most of them will be sitting up and starting to take notice.'

'Even the serious ones?'

'We don't hang about these days, you know. Even heart transplant patients tend to be up and about within about twenty-four hours.'

'What about the empty beds?'

'Ah, those who can get around usually wander off to the day room to watch TV. Which reminds

me; when we've finished here, could you scoot over
and track down Mr Jennings? The new chap will
want to examine him and Staff will expect to see
him sitting in his place all neatly scrubbed and
polished at the appropriate time.'

Pippa looked at him, never quite sure whether he
was being serious or not. 'You're joking.'

He took pity on her. 'Yes, of course I am. All the
same, he'll need to be here. He had his op ten days
ago and with a bit of luck should be discharged any
day now, so you'll find he'll probably come quite
willingly. Actually, you can go now. I'll finish here.'

'But what about Staff?'

'Don't you worry about that. I can handle
Cynthia Baker.'

Pippa hesitated, then went, deciding he probably
could. There was something very nice about Pete
Gibson, if one didn't take him at all seriously.

She found the day room where a dozen patients,
male and female, were ensconced in front of a
television set, some chatting, some smoking, some
dozing.

'Er . . . Mr Jennings?' she enquired hopefully.
The lack of response was daunting. She tried again.
'Mr Jennings?'

'Ssh.' A ring of faces turned resentfully from the
day's main race at Catterick and she blushed. This
was ridiculous. Drawing herself up to her full
height, she scanned the group. 'I'm sorry, but Mr
Jennings is wanted on Men's Surgical, as soon as
possible please.'

One wag looked up at her pink face and grinned.
'Need 'im to perform an emergency op do you,
Nurse? I'll just tell 'im and he can go and get his
scalpel sharpened. 'Ere, Alf,' he aimed a half-

hearted kick at the man snoring in the chair opposite. 'You're needed on Men's Surgical. There's a crisis and you're needed to save the day.'

'Oh Gawd.' The figure emerged, grumpily. 'The one time I get a decent kip in this place and they have to wake me up. Staff cracking the whip again, is she?' He got to his feet, fastening his dressing-gown. 'That woman's got no soul.'

Pippa hid an inclination to agree. 'I'm sorry, Mr Jennings, but the consultant is due to make his round soon and you'll need his blessing before we can let you go, so I should humour her if I were you, just this once.'

He walked beside her back to the ward, slippers flapping, dressing-gown held together by a frayed cord and pyjamas by sheer will-power. Staff would have a field day.

'Student, aren't you? Let loose on the ward for your first stint at the real stuff?'

She felt deflated. So much for her carefully nurtured air of confidence that the uniform would fool anyone. 'Is it really so obvious?'

'Naw. Don't let it bother you. I've been reading the booklet they hand out.'

'Oh.' That was slightly cheering.

'Anyway, I expect the manner comes with experience. Give it a few more years and you'll be just like Staff Nurse Baker.'

Her horrified gaze flew up just in time to catch his broad wink.

'What's the new fellow like, anyway?'

'I really don't know,' she had to admit.

'I bet he'll have you girls fighting over him in no time. It's the white coats, I expect.'

She tried to look cross. 'Mr Jennings, where do

you get these ideas? He's probably ninety if he's a day, and besides,' she spoilt the effect by giggling, 'consultants rarely wear white coats. I expect it's because they can afford decent suits.'

Staff Nurse Baker clearly didn't share her good humour as she came down the ward like a ship in full sail. 'Nurse Benedict, just what do you think you're doing leaving this ward and wandering about the hospital without permission?'

'But, Staff . . .'

'I don't have time to listen to excuses, Nurse.' Pale grey eyes beamed disapproval. 'Mr Jennings, if you could possibly remain where we can find you, at least for the next half-hour, I would be most grateful.'

There was a sudden flurry of activity as the swing doors opened and Pippa caught a glimpse of a dark, immaculate suit just as Staff's fingers jabbed her painfully in the back. 'Oh my goodness, he's here. Go, Nurse, at once. Remove yourself and that bag of soiled linen and stay out of sight, on pain of death, do you hear? Nurse Gibson, go and tell Sister that Mr Sterling is here. Wretched man. Doesn't he know he's early? Move, Nurse, move.'

Pippa moved, flinging a look of furious resentment over her shoulder at the distant figure surrounded by a solemn-faced retinue who clearly shared Staff's view that he was one of the precious few. She reached the sluice muttering crossly, to be joined a few seconds later by Liz, who was looking equally thunderous.

'Well thank heavens you're here too. I was beginning to think it was just me when Staff came along and ordered me out of sight.'

Pippa disposed of the black plastic sack of linen

with a fury which didn't even begin to take the edge off the resentment she was feeling.

'Apparently,' her mouth compressed, 'we are both unfit to be seen by the eyes of the precious consultant. I think this is crazy. Sister Tutor didn't tell it by half. I'm having most of my illusions shattered right here on the ward, and this is not my idea of nursing, having to skulk in the sluice while the great man does his round.'

'What do they think we'll do, anyway?'

'I know what I'd like to do.'

They both stared dejectedly at the clinically white walls, the stainless steel—and at each other. 'How are you getting on, anyway?'

Liz shrugged. 'I don't know. It's not quite what I expected.'

'No, I know what you mean. I'm not sure what I expected, but this certainly isn't it. Pippa contemplated the door. 'Did you get a look at him?'

'Who?'

'*Him*, idiot.'

'Oh no. No such luck. One minute I was tidying lockers, the next I was in here.'

'Hm, I know the feeling. I may have a broken rib to prove it.' Pippa probed the bruise where Staff Nurse Baker's fingers had made contact and winced. 'How long do you suppose we're meant to lurk in here?'

'How long does a round take?'

'I've no idea. It wasn't one of the things Sister Tutor covered.' Pippa frowned and moved to the door. 'I wonder what he's like.'

'Probably ten feet tall.'

Pippa laughed softly. 'Well, I don't see why we had to be banished. I mean, sooner or later they're going to have to let us behave like real nurses, aren't they?'

Liz looked at her fob watch. 'I don't think Staff sees anyone who hasn't actually qualified as a real nurse, and even then I have my doubts. Unfortunately, when she ordered me out I made the mistake of arguing, which probably means I'm in for a hard time from now on. "Until I can trust you, Nurse,"' she mimicked, '"not to do something diabolical." Presumably she means like showing my naked hands to a consultant. "You will stay out of sight. We will discuss it later."' Liz sighed. 'Why, what have you heard about the new man?'

'Nothing, except that his name is Sterling.'

'What, you mean not pure gold?' Liz chuckled. 'I heard that he's spent some time in Canada and he's gaining quite a reputation for himself in heart cases.'

'Well he isn't doing much for mine right now. I'm gasping for a cup of tea. I wonder if he's gone yet? I'm going to have a peep.'

'I wouldn't if I were you. If you get caught, Sister will have your head, or worse.'

Liz's warning was ignored as Pippa opened the door a crack and peered out. 'I'm only looking.'

'Curiosity killed the cat.' Liz came to stand beside her. 'What can you see?'

'Nothing. Just a head above the crowd. At least he's not old.'

'How can you possibly tell?'

'His hair is black, not grey.' Pippa felt a slightly odd sensation run through her and dismissed it as nothing more than nerves. After all, why should the mere sight of the back of someone's head make her feel . . . threatened? 'They've gathered round one of the beds. I can see Sister.' She paused. 'Oh lor.'

'What is it?'

Pippa drew back fractionally. 'Oh no. It's Mr Tate. He's seen me.' She stared at the stout figure gesturing wildly in her direction from the bed opposite.

'Nurse!' he hissed. 'Nurse, I need a bedpan.'

'Oh, not now, Mr Tate,' she muttered pleadingly under her breath, and held up her hand. 'Please, not now.'

'But, Nurse, I can't wait.'

She shrank back into the room, closing her eyes. 'He wants a bedpan.'

'Well can't he wait?'

'From the looks of him I doubt it. He's getting very red in the face. I wouldn't like him to burst a blood vessel—or anything else come to that.'

'So what are you going to do? You know we're not supposed to be on the ward.'

'What *can* I do? I can't just leave him like that.' She groaned. 'I'll have to get one. Perhaps no one will notice if I creep across.'

'I wouldn't count on it.' Liz opened the door herself. 'What about Pete Gibson? Why isn't he around?'

'He went down to X-ray with a patient. It's no good. I'll have to go.'

'I think you're right. Mr Tate is practically in tears.'

Pippa drew herself up decisively. 'Where are they kept?'

'Through there, I think.'

She collected the item, covering the cold plastic with a cloth, took a deep breath and opened the door. The group were still gathered around one of the beds. She could hear the hum of voices. One, male, above the rest seemed to stir some vague memory as she caught Mr Tate's plaintive cry of, 'Nurse!'

She put her finger imploringly to her lips. 'I'm coming, Mr Tate. Are you absolutely sure you can't wait?'

He gave a strangled cry and she darted a helpless glance along the ward for some sign of Pete Gibson. He was obviously still down in X-ray. There was no help for it. Taking her courage and the bedpan in both hands, she let the door of the sluice room close quietly behind her and started across the ward.

With her eye fixed firmly on Sister's bobbing white cap, Pippa headed towards the bed and Mr Tate, who was struggling frantically to draw the curtains round his predicament in the certain hope that relief was on its way.

Her brain mentally registered the tiny wet patch on the floor just seconds before her foot hit it. By then, of course, it was too late. She caught a brief glimpse of the patient's startled face as her feet shot in all directions, the look of agonised despair on Mr Tate's features almost laughable, and wished she could die as the bedpan clattered to the floor and skidded along, hitting the metal bed-rail and performed an ear-shattering, dervish-like spin until it came to rest in front of one of the beds.

As if everything was suddenly happening in slow motion, she was on her knees as the group turned. She caught a vague impression of horror on Staff Nurse Baker's face as she tried to struggle to her feet and found the heel of her shoe caught in her dress. Even Mr Tate's cry of anguish might have

been funny, except that she hadn't the slightest
inclination to laugh, or do anything except die of
mortification at that precise moment. Her cheeks
were scarlet and her eyes stinging with tears as
Sister's voice closed in over her.

'Nurse, what are you doing?'

From the floor, where she was struggling to
disentangle her foot from her hem, she gasped, 'I
was just . . . Mr Tate needed a bedpan, Sister.' Her
voice sounded hysterical and she closed her eyes as
the spectacle of the upturned bedpan floated
in front of them, and opened them again to discover a pair of male feet planted firmly in front of
her.

'Perhaps I can help?'

Her gaze travelled upwards over a pair of trou-
sered legs which seemed to go on for ever, and
finally came to rest with a deepening sense of
foreboding on an unsmiling, masculine face. There
should have been some comfort in the total absence
of recognition on his part, if her own stupefied
brain hadn't known exactly what colour his eyes
would be, precisely where the tiny cleft in his chin
was, and precisely where she had last seen Mr
Julius Sterling!

Pippa battled with a sudden and overwhelming
urge to burst into tears as she prayed he wouldn't
remember. Her mouth quivered as the colour
surged painfully into her cheeks beneath the dis-
turbingly cool appraisal, and she knew it had to be a
vain hope as the memory of the long, slim hands
brushing against her skin drifted back to haunt her.
The way he had let her go on chattering so naively,
and all the time he had known. No doubt thought
the whole thing a huge joke at her expense. Well,

it wasn't funny. She swallowed hard. She would never forgive him.

'Are you all right? Not hurt?'

She realised with a start that his hand was still on her arm and released herself quickly as Staff Nurse Baker glared furiously in her direction. 'Yes, thank you, I'm fine.' No thanks to you, she thought. Fine, if she discounted the fact that her knees were throbbing and that she would never, never get over the awful humiliation. 'Fine,' she muttered again. 'I slipped.'

He studied her, frowning, for a long moment before he nodded.

'As long as no harm is done and it doesn't become a habit. I prefer, if possible, to conduct my rounds in relative calm and quiet.'

Pippa's mouth opened on a protest, only to find that he was already striding away. Which was probably as well, since she was fighting an almost childish urge to inform him that, contrary to his obvious beliefs, she did not make a habit of throwing herself at the knees of consultants. It was left to Staff Nurse Baker to round on her furiously and hiss, 'Pick up that bedpan, Nurse. Attend to Mr Tate and report to Sister's office when the round is over.'

Pippa glared after the retreating figure through a mist of angry tears before she turned blindly away and drew the curtains around Mr Tate's bed. His own remorse, if anything, made things worse as he stumbled over an apology.

'I'm sorry, Nurse. It was all my fault. The last thing I wanted was to get you in trouble.'

She felt instantly contrite and ashamed. 'No, Mr Tate, of course you weren't to blame. It was an accident. that's all.' She offered the quick reassurance and was glad to see that he accepted it, even if a little warily.

'You won't get a telling off, will you? That Staff Nurse is a right tartar. I wouldn't fancy tangling with her myself.'

Pippa summoned a smile as she drew back the curtains. 'No, I shouldn't think so. Anyway, I'm a big girl now you know. Quite able to take care of myself.'

He still looked doubtful. 'Well, you all look scraps of things to me. Far too young for so much responsibility.'

She felt like saying, 'But we grow up fast,' but didn't as she made him comfortable again and emerged from behind the curtains in time to see the back of Julius Sterling's tall figure striding from the ward. Suddenly she felt very tired and depressed without really knowing why. Perhaps it was because she sensed that somehow the new consultant cardiologist was going to cause far more trouble in her life than Staff Nurse Baker ever could. And to make things worse, he probably regarded her as a prize idiot who wasn't capable of performing even the most minor task without causing confusion.

And he's probably right, she thought dejectedly, as she rushed into the sluice yet again, reminding herself crossly that she didn't really care what Mr Julius Sterling thought.

CHAPTER THREE

PIPPA glanced up at the darkening sky, huddling deeper into her cloak as she ran down the steps to where Liz was waiting, her face wearing a noticeable look of apprehension as she fell into step beside her.

'I thought you were never going to get away. Well, what happened? Oh damn, here comes the rain. Come on, let's run for the car.'

They reached the ancient but lovingly preserved Morris Minor just as the skies opened, and leapt inside, breathing hard as they shed their cloaks. 'So come on, tell me,' Liz reiterated, inserting the key in the ignition.

Pippa shrugged. 'Nothing happened.'

'What do you mean, nothing?'

'Just that. I hung around for the rest of the afternoon outside Sister's office but she was busy elsewhere, at a meeting or something, and Staff went to tea, and by the time I was finally called in, all Sister said was, "I'm sure you acted from the best of motives, Nurse, but in future no matter how well-intentioned, you must not take it upon yourself to disobey Staff's instructions."'

Liz stared disbelievingly. 'So what were you supposed to do? Let the poor man burst?'

'Apparently Mr Tate should have rung his bell for one of the other nurses to attend to him.'

'Well you could hardly know that.'

Pippa shrugged unhappily. 'Perhaps I should.

Anyway, I do now and I'm certainly not likely to forget in a hurry. Come to think of it, nor is Mr Sterling,' she added miserably as Liz started the car and headed out into the traffic.

'Well, I think it's very odd. I was sure you were in for a rocket. Do you think he could have said anything to Sister?'

Pippa snorted. 'Nothing in my favour, that's for sure. He's not the sort.'

'I thought he looked rather dishy.'

'Well that just goes to show how looks can deceive,' came the hot retort. 'I'm quite sure behind those cold grey eyes there beats an equally cold heart.'

'Oh, you did notice then? His eyes, I mean.' She saw Pippa's lips tighten and chuckled. 'Well, apart from the fact that he could stun me with a single glance, I think you're being a bit hard. I mean, I can appreciate there was a certain loss of dignity involved, but you can hardly blame him for that.'

'Oh yes I can.' Pippa turned to stare miserably out of the window. 'What I didn't have time to tell you was that he's the one. The man I told you about. The one I thought was visiting a patient in the private wing.'

Liz's gaze swerved from the road. 'You're kidding?'

'I wish I was.' Pippa blinked hard and tried to swallow the sudden lump in her throat. 'What I can't forgive is that he was quite happy to let me go on making a fool of myself, knowing all the time that . . .' She sniffed. 'I think he's despicable. God knows I'll never be able to face him again, not that I would want to.'

'That may be a bit difficult, don't you think,

when it looks as if he's all set to become part of the establishment? And from what I hear, Clem's is jolly lucky to get him.'

'Ha, and I don't doubt he'll see to it that he's appreciated to the full,' Pippa said scathingly. She refused to be impressed. In her book Julius Sterling was deceitful, arrogant and thoroughly overbearing. She chewed at her lip, a niggling suspicion that she was perhaps being slightly unfair pushed away, along with a nasty thought that he was also the kind of man some women might find very attractive. But then, there was no accounting for taste.

'What you need is a good strong cup of tea and some nice thick toast with layers of strawberry jam.' Liz was a great believer in the efficacies of food for lessening life's trouble. 'Why don't I make it, then we can go out for half an hour's brisk walk before we make a start on that essay for Sister Tutor.'

'Oh no.' Pippa slid down in the seat. 'I'd forgotten all about it. You know, right now I'm wondering why I ever decided I wanted to be a nurse. I must have been mad.'

'You're tired, that's all.'

But was that true? Pippa wondered, staring unseeingly at the passing traffic. Right now all she could think of was that her head ached, her legs ached and somehow her first day on the ward hadn't come anywhere near her expectations. She didn't even feel like a nurse.

'We just have to convince ourselves it can only get better,' Liz tried cheerfully, and lapsed into her own weary silence. 'At least tomorrow is Tuesday.'

'So wake me when it's Sunday.'

It seemed like a good idea to which nothing could

be added, and nothing else was said until the tea had been poured and a pile of toast had disappeared. Pippa sat back, trying desperately to keep her eyes open.

'I know I'm definitely not going to survive this course. This is only my first day on the ward and I can't think of a single place on my body that doesn't ache. I'm dead beat. Staff Nurse Baker hates me and I've managed to make myself public enemy number one with the new consultant.'

'Well that's not bad going for the first day.' Liz stretched and groaned. 'And what exactly did you have in mind for tomorrow, Nurse Benedict?'

'I thought possibly resignation.' Pippa stared at the ceiling. 'Diplomatic retreat.'

'Cowardice, sheer cowardice. You're not serious?'

'Right now, absolutely. Oh, I don't know. Well, you have to admit it's tempting. As it is, it's far more likely a case of whether I'm allowed to stay—and if Mr Sterling has anything to do with it, I should think my days are already numbered.' She sat back, arms crossed behind her head. 'I wonder what he's really like?'

'Who?'

'Him, idiot.'

Liz pulled a face. 'Probably married with at least three children.'

Pippa closed her eyes, wondering why the idea should be vaguely displeasing, and told herself sharply that she really wasn't interested in Julius Sterling's private life anyway, just as long as he didn't interfere too much in her own.

'Personally I think you're being over-sensitive on all counts. Accidents happen and I can't honestly

see any consultants indulging in a personal ven-
detta, especially not against someone as junior as
we are. They live on a far higher plain than this, my
child. Sister Tutor was right. They don't even
recognise the lower forms of life. Of which,' Liz
yawned, 'after today I know I am most definitely
one.' She lowered her feet from a stool. 'It's depressing, isn't it?'

Pippa eyed the tray of dirty dishes and decided
she hadn't the energy to move. 'I could rapidly lose
what little self-confidence I ever had. On the other
hand,' she got to her feet with a groan, 'this is no
good. I've got to make a start on that essay or I'll
never get it done in time. The question is, how do I
fill twenty pages on the sterile procedure for dressing a wound?'

'Don't ask me. I was just having the same
thought about filling ten. Frankly, Benedict, there
are times when I wonder why I'm still your friend.'
It was said with a grin which took any seriousness
out of it, but the air was still heavy with tension for
the next two hours, broken only by an occasional
groan and the scratching of pens as they worked.

'Well that's it.' Pippa sat back to stare, bleary-
eyed, at the cup of cocoa that was put in front of
her.

'Finished?'

'As finished as it's ever likely to be. I couldn't
squeeze another line out of it if I tried, so Sister is
going to have to settle for eighteen and a half
pages.'

'I don't suppose she'll even count.'

'What time is it?'

'Just gone eleven.'

'What?'

Liz yawned. 'I wondered if you'd noticed.'

'Well that settles it. I'm off to bed. If I have to face another day like today I need all the sleep I can get, and then some.'

Which made it all the more annoying that when Pippa finally climbed in between the sheets she found herself thinking of Julius Sterling, as he had been before she knew who he was! She thumped the pillows hard and snuggled under the covers.

There was a distinctly noticeable lack of tension in the air as she walked on to Men's Surgical next morning, probably due, as Anne Roberts the second-year confided as they met in the kitchen, to the fact that it was Staff Nurse Baker's day off.

Pippa couldn't help the tiny bubble of relief which welled up and immediately felt guilty as Anne laughed. 'You're not the only one who feels that way, believe me. I don't know why it is. I'm sure she doesn't intend it, but you can almost feel everyone relax when they know she isn't going to be around.'

'It can't be exactly good for morale.' Pippa loaded cups on to the trolley for the breakfasts which were about to be served. 'So why is she allowed to get away with it?'

'Oh, I don't know. I think her manner is unfortunate rather than malicious. She's a good nurse and the patients probably appreciate the fact. Most of them aren't here long enough to become too bothered by it, anyway, lucky things. As for the rest of us, well, she tends to concentrate her venom on the newest recruit.'

'You mean it looks as if I'm it.' The thought wasn't exactly cheering.

Anne smiled. 'Don't let it get you down. You

won't be here that long, and as soon as the next bunch of students arrive she'll pick on one of them. The trick is to keep out of her way as much as possible, and it's easier to do than you might think Just find something to do when she's around. If you can't find anything, invent it. As long as you look reasonably busy you're probably safe.'

'Thanks for the tip. I'll remember it.'

'Okay. But if in doubt you can always go to Pete Gibson. As a nurse he's first class—but be warned, you'd be well-advised to keep things on a strictly business level. Unless, of course, you happen to like the type.'

'No thanks. He moves a bit too quickly for me.'

'That's the general opinion.' Anne smiled. 'He has a reputation, richly deserved I might add, as something of a philanderer.'

Pippa raised an eyebrow. 'I hadn't heard exactly, but I'd guessed.'

'Yes, well it's early days. You can take it from me, there's not a nurse at Clem's who hasn't found herself locked in the linen cupboard or sluice with that particular young man at some time or other. 'Not,' she added with a twinkle in her eye, 'that I'm saying most of them haven't enjoyed the experience enormously. Our Mr Gibson hath a certain charm. I'm not quite sure what it is, it's certainly not his plausibility. You can't take anything he says seriously.'

'I had noticed.'

'I thought I'd just let you know, that's all.'

'Well, thanks for the warning. I appreciate it.'

Anne smiled. 'Right now we'd better get these breakfasts out. Sister Carson is very nice, but there's a routine to follow and it's best for all of us if we keep to it. It only needs one little incident to put us out for the rest of the day. You'll soon get the hang of it. Come on, you push the trolley and I'll show you who has what.'

'But how on earth do you remember it all?'

'You don't. Here, you start pouring the teas, will you? Patients are given a menu and they tick what they want, then it goes down to the catering staff. You simply have to consult your list, and it's important that you do. Some are on restricted diets, which means they aren't allowed certain foods, and you have to watch them. Some of them don't have many scruples about it if they think they can get away with it. Others, like Mr Hill for instance, Mr James, next to him, and Mr Winter, aren't having breakfast at all today.'

'Why is that?'

'Well, you'll see on your list and above those beds, it says "nil by mouth". That's because those patients are due for ops this morning and if they were given food the op would have to be cancelled. Which wouldn't make you the most popular person in anyone's book, so always check. I expect you covered this in PTS though?'

They had. The funny thing was though that it was one thing to discuss the various procedures in the safety of the lecture room, but things took on a quite different perspective when it came to the real thing.

Seeing her confusion, Anne took pity. 'Don't worry about it. For the first few weeks it's all a bit terrifying. You think you'll never learn it all but you do, gradually, and probably without even realising it. In any case, you won't be asked to do anything you haven't covered or aren't capable of.

The system works pretty well in that respect.'

Feeling only slightly reassured, Pippa handed out tea, drew up bed-tables for those patients not allowed out of bed, and distributed plates of bacon and sausage.

Breakfasts over, the trolley was wheeled away and the first patient went up to Theatre. Sister Carson spent some time chatting to the man, explaining the procedures once again and doing her best to put his mind at rest. 'I expect you're feeling a little drowsy, Mr Hill. That's the pre-med working.'

'I feel fine, Sister.'

'Good. In a few minutes the porters will wheel you up to Theatre where you'll be given an injection. I promise you, the next thing you know you'll be back here in your bed and soon feeling much better.' She glanced up at Pippa, a smile emphasising the attractiveness of her features. 'Perhaps you'd like Nurse to go with you?'

Pippa stared, horrified. 'But I . . .'

Sister smiled. 'Don't worry, Nurse. All you have to do is accompany Mr Hills in the lift to Theatre, nothing more. I'm sure you can manage that.'

Pippa blinked, pleased. 'Oh yes, of course I can, Sister.' She smiled down at the man who closed his eyes in apparent unawareness that he was being trusted to a raw student who had scarcely been allowed near a patient before, let alone taken one to Theatre.

'Good.' Sister walked away hiding a smile. Her own student days weren't so far behind that she couldn't remember the awful mingling of terror one minute and pride the next, and Nurse Benedict's face had brought it all rushing back. 'You have

about fifteen minutes before the trolley arrives,
Nurse. Perhaps you'd give Nurse Gibson a hand.
All the beds have to be stripped and re-made. It
shouldn't take long.'

Pippa swallowed hard. 'All of them, Sister?'

'That's right, Nurse. Collect the clean linen from
the cupboard, will you, and load it on to the trolley.
When you've taken Mr Hill up to Theatre you can
go to coffee. You have twenty minutes. Make sure
you get back on time.'

'Yes, Sister.'

'When you get back you can give a hand with the
blanket baths. Have you done one before?'

Pippa gulped. 'Only in PTS, Sister.'

'Well we all have to start on the real thing sooner
or later. It's really quite easy.'

All the same, Pippa couldn't help wishing it was
later, much later, as she finally rushed down to the
cafeteria for coffee, wondering how she was going
to get through the rest of the day at such a hectic
pace.

Pete Gibson saw her looking hot and harassed
and took pity, bringing her a cup of coffee with his
own. Detaching himself from the queue, he sat at
the table, pushing the cup towards her and ladling
sugar into his own.

'Oh, bless you. When I saw that queue I thought
I was going to have to resign myself to going
without.'

'Heaven forbid! A Nurse lives on her feet and
cups of coffee. Not that I intend making a habit of
this, but you look as if you need it.'

'You have no idea.'

He grinned. 'Hard going, is it?'

She nodded over the cup. 'How do you survive?

The morning's only half gone and I'm exhausted. It never stops, does it?'

'You get used to it. Actually it does ease up occasionally, at visiting times for instance, but you'll probably have the flowers to do and the afternoon teas to give out and clear away.'

'Oh, thanks.'

'All part of the service.' He rested his elbows on the table and looked at her with a gleam in his eye. 'You made quite an impression on our Mr Sterling yesterday, so I hear.'

Pippa choked on her coffee and put the cup hastily back on the saucer. 'Don't. I'm trying to forget. It was the most embarrassing moment of my life.'

'Oh come on, don't take it so seriously. It's not as if any real harm was done. In fact I heard it was actually quite funny.'

'Hm, well Staff Baker certainly didn't think so, and I had to report to Sister.'

'Ah yes, but then Baker has no sense of humour. Still, I suppose you might be wise to steer clear of the great man himself for a while. Until he's forgotten.'

She didn't answer. Somehow she had the feeling that her face was probably indelibly imprinted on Julius Sterling's mind for ever.

'What are you doing tonight?' Pete asked.

She blushed at the unexpectedness of the question. 'I don't know. Studying, I suppose. Why?'

'How about coming out for a drink? Take your mind off all this. Apart from that, it helps to get rid of the smell of antiseptic for a while.'

She toyed with the spoon, feeling the heat gather

in her cheeks. She was tempted, as much by the offer of escape as by a curious desire to know what Pete was really like. That was the odd thing about uniforms, they tended to deprive the wearer of any kind of individuality, yet something told her that an evening spent in Pete Gibson's company wouldn't be entirely dull.

She caught the gleam in his eye and retreated to the safer ground of common sense. Life was quite complicated enough at the moment.

She got to her feet looking at her watch. 'It's a nice thought, but I'd better not. I've masses of written work to hand in to Sister Tutor.'

'Chicken,' he teased. 'Or do I take it my reputation has gone before? You don't want to believe all you hear, you know.'

She blushed furiously. 'Not at all. I'm just saying that now isn't really a good time. Our reports will be made up soon, and frankly I'm not in with a chance of being student of the year. Perhaps some other time?'

'Count on it.'

Did she detect just a tiny note of regret in his voice? 'Look, I really do have to get back. Are you coming up to the ward?'

'Later, I'm collecting a patient from X-ray first.'

She left the crowded cafeteria and ran lightly up the stairs to get back to the ward just within the allotted time, but only just.

After that it was a mad race to finish the blanket baths, and it wasn't until they were over that Pippa realised she had managed to get through them without even the slightest feeling of embarrassment. 'Too busy keeping an eye on the time,' Liz whispered as they passed each other going in opposite directions. 'Do you suppose it's always as busy as this?'

'I hope not. I'll never survive.'

'Come along, Nurses.' Sister Carson's voice intruded sharply as she poked her head round the kitchen door. 'We have a patient coming back from Theatre and another to go down. None of us have time to stand gossiping.'

'Yes, Sister.' They fled, and the rest of the morning disappeared in a haze of swabbing lockers, watching treatments, learning how to dispense the four-hourly medicines and generally scurrying to the sluice with bedpans and soiled laundry.

It came as something of a shock to hear Sister saying, 'Right, Nurse Benedict, off you go to lunch now. You have an hour. Kindly take at least five minutes of it to make sure your appearance is neat and tidy before you come back, and don't be late. Other people have to have lunch and it's visitors at three.' She was gone, leaving them to fly in the direction of the cafeteria and join the inevitable queue.

Trays finally laden with mounds of shepherd's pie and rhubarb crumble, they edged their way towards the table where Jane Greaves was beckoning to them.

'Hi. I was hoping I'd see someone from the set.'

'You're on your own.'

'Yes, I know, and it's horrid. In fact I nearly skipped lunch, but my stomach is rattling so loudly Sister would be bound to notice.'

Pippa unloaded her tray and eased herself into the seat. 'But where's Patterson? I thought you and he both went up to Women's Med?' She added a generous helping of brown sauce and caught Jane's eye. 'It helps disguise the flavour.'

'Yes, well we did, but Sister told him to take second lunch. To be honest, I think she fancies him.'

'What, Rick?'

'Well why not? He's not bad, you know. Quite nice in fact.'

'Oh well, everyone to their own taste I suppose.' Pippa stabbed a lump of solid potato. 'You could say the same about this meal. If I wasn't so hungry I'd protest.'

'It wouldn't get you anywhere, so save your breath.' Liz stared at her own plate with obvious misgivings. 'And don't forget we've got about half an hour left.'

'How about you?' Jane asked. 'What's Surgical like?'

'Not so bad really. Hectic. Staff Nurse Baker keeps everyone in a state of rigid tension but Carson is nice. I'm surprised she isn't married.'

'She's engaged, I heard. To one of the housemen I think. Mike Harris.'

'Don't know him.'

'No, well we don't move in quite those exalted circles yet, do we, and aren't ever likely to, according to Sister Tutor.' Jane sighed.

'What's the matter? Not having any luck catching a handsome doctor in a white coat?'

'Ha, I should be so lucky! The only man I've seen in a white coat so far was sixty if he's a day.'

'You should ask Benedict here if you need any advice. She rather favours the drastic approach, but I must admit it seems to work,' Liz laughed.

Pippa threw her a look of disgust. 'Do you have

to remind me? Do you want me to have indigestion for the rest of the day?'

'So what's this then?'

'Oh, just that our Benedict seems to have fallen rather heavily for the new cardiologist, Mr Sterling, you might say.' Liz chuckled at the glare aimed in her direction.

'If you must know, I'm getting sick of the sound of his name.'

'Then you must be the only female at Clem's who is. He's gorgeous.' Jane leaned across the table. 'The girls have already nicknamed him Bachelor of Hearts. Lucky you.' Her eyes gleamed speculatively in Pippa's direction. 'Perhaps I should ask for a transfer.'

'I wouldn't bother. He's really the most arrogant, impossible . . .'

'You'll gather he made quite an impression.'

Pippa gave her attention to her pudding, only to jerk up sharply at the thought that she would far rather have made a very different impression upon Mr Julius Sterling. She swallowed her hot coffee. 'Anyway, what do you think of it all so far?'

'It's not so bad really.'

'I keep telling myself I won't always be making beds and dishing out bedpans.'

'I wouldn't count on that for at least the next three years. You know what they say. RHIP.'

They both stared at Liz.

'Rank hath its privileges.'

They lapsed into glum silence for another five minutes until Jane moved reluctantly, gathering up her bag. 'Well, I'm off. If I sit here any longer I shall fall asleep.'

'Hang on, we'll come with you.' It was the end of

a brief escape. 'We'd better pop into the cloak-room, anyway. I don't suppose you've got a spare pair of tights, have you?'

'Here, you can have these, but let me have them back on pay day. I get through dozens and they're costing me a small fortune.'

They trooped back up the stairs together, emerging minutes later to go their separate ways.

Sister went for her own lunch leaving Pete Gibson to cover. He was a good nurse. The patients obviously liked his easy manner which seemed to get even the most unpleasant of tasks performed with as little hindrance or discomfort as possible, Pippa had noticed. It occurred to her to wonder, as she went to ask what she should do, that he hadn't chosen to become a doctor rather than a nurse. A question answered not entirely seriously, she suspected, as he took a temperature and charted the results before guiding her to the office.

'Didn't fancy it.' He lounged in Sister's chair in a way that had Pippa darting nervous glances in the direction of the window in case Sister should reappear. Not, she thought, that Pete wasn't perfectly capable of charming Sister as well. 'Look, for heaven's sake, relax for a minute! This is as quiet as we're ever likely to get and you have to learn to make the most of it. Sit down.'

She sat on the edge of the chair, hands clasped in her lap, and he grinned. 'You'll end up a nervous wreck. Don't take it all so seriously, my sweet.'

'But it *is* serious,' she protested, pretending she hadn't heard the endearment. 'I know it may not seem like it, but I really do want to get through my training and qualify, and it's all right for you. Your exams are over.'

His eyebrows lifted slightly. 'They may be over. I still have to wait for the results.'

'Oh yes, but you'll pass.'

He laughed softly as he got to his feet and moved to the cabinet behind her. 'Thank you for those few kind words. It's nice to know you care.'

Pippa had the feeling that the conversation was moving in an entirely different direction. 'Well, of course you will. You obviously love the work, so why did you choose not to become a medical student?'

'Like I said, no inclination, no staying power. No ambition. Seven years of hard slog isn't for me. I'm basically quite lazy at heart, and it takes a certain degree of dedication to qualify—or hadn't you noticed? All that studying can play havoc with a man's love-life, you know.'

She realised he was teasing and resisted the urge to respond. 'You're incorrigible.'

'And you're very sweet.'

Before Pippa realised what was happening, he had kissed her suddenly on the lips. She was held rigid by shock as much as the fact that his arms were encircling her waist, pulling her towards him. The realisation that Sister or any one of the other members of staff might walk in lent a kind of desperation to her struggles, which seemed to be having remarkably little effect—until the voice, coming from the doorway, brought the charade to an end far more quickly and brutally than she had anticipated. She was released so quickly, cheeks scarlet, that she might have fallen if she hadn't managed to hold on to a chair for support.

'If it's not causing too much inconvenience, I would like to see Sister.'

Pippa was aware of a penetrating stare which took in every traitorous detail of her dishevelled appearance, from her cap, which had been knocked sideways, to the burning of her cheeks, heightened, she told herself crossly, by a totally irrational feeling of guilt. Her mouth compressed as she met the stare. After all, she hadn't been the one to start it. Not that Julius Sterling would concern himself with a simple fact like that. It was some consolation to see that Pete had the grace to look sheepish as he said gruffly, 'Sir?'

The dark eyes left her face, but not before she had caught the sudden tightening of the muscles of his jaw which told her that he had drawn his own conclusions from the scene—and for some reason the knowledge left her feeling hurt and angry. Her mouth opened on a protest, but he had already dismissed her from his mind.

'Perhaps you can tell me where I might find Sister?'

'I'm afraid she's gone to lunch, sir. I'm in charge at the moment.'

Julius Sterling's eyebrows moved impressively. 'I don't doubt it. However, perhaps when she returns you'd be good enough to tell her that I shall have to take my round fifteen minutes early tomorrow morning in order to fit in a clinic.'

'Yes, sir. I'll tell her as soon as she comes back to the ward.'

It was galling to see Pete regain his composure so rapidly. It would have been nice to say the same for herself, but her heart was thudding erratically and wasn't helped by the long, cool look which left her feeling faint.

'I don't believe I actually know your name.'

Pippa swallowed hard, aware exactly why he must want to know and furious with herself for not having foreseen what would happen. She lowered her gaze. 'Benedict, sir. Student Nurse Benedict.' Waiting for the inevitable wrath to descend, she battled with the lump in her throat and thought, 'it's all so unfair.' It was some seconds before she realised that he had turned abruptly on his heel and marched through the door, leaving her to sag weakly against the desk.

'Phew, that was close.'

To her annoyance Pete even managed a grin, which made her want to hit him.

'You . . . you idiot!'

'Look,' he laughed, 'it's not that bad. I don't suppose he actually saw anything, and even if he did it wasn't exactly compromising, was it?'

Pippa could hardly speak for the fury which seemed to have engulfed her. 'Wasn't it?' She knew she was being unreasonable, but tried to see it through the eyes of Julius Sterling—and didn't like what she saw.

She moved quickly to the door, flinging a look of reproach in Pete's direction. 'I have to get back.'

To her dismay he barred her exit. 'Look, I really am sorry, but I think you're making too much of it.'

'Do you?' Her temper flared. 'Well, perhaps you should have thought of that before you . . . before you . . .' Tears stung her eyes and she blinked them away. 'I suppose you realise I'll probably be out of a job.'

'What, just because of a kiss? Dear girl, aren't you being very naive? Even Sterling must be human. Besides, why do I get to take all the blame? I don't think you know precisely what kind of effect you have on a man.'

She retreated huffily from his grasp. 'Well I certainly know precisely what effect I have on Mr Sterling, thanks to you. I don't believe you take anything seriously.'

'You'd be surprised. Beneath all this show and bravado I'm really quite a nice guy when you get to know me better.'

She side-stepped him neatly and wrenched the door open. 'Thanks for the offer, but I don't think I want to get to know you better, Mr Gibson. I can't afford to, not if I want to keep my job.'

Surprisingly enough, however, it wasn't her job she was thinking about as she marched along the ward. She was far more concerned with the un-answerable question of why it should bother her so much what Julius Sterling had thought.

Her eyes half-closed on a thought so fleeting, so impossible, that it was gone even before she recognised it.

CHAPTER FOUR

THE TEMPO quickened again as Sister returned from her own lunch. Patients woke from after-lunch naps and looked forward to the arrival of afternoon visitors. There were TPRs to be done, medicines to be given out and post-op patients to be constantly checked. Added to which was the uncomfortable awareness that Sister Tutor would expect a well-written, lengthy essay on their first experience of working on a ward.

Liz, coming into the kitchen to hunt for extra flower vases, leaned wearily against the sink. 'I sometimes get the feeling it would be better to drop out at this stage rather than struggle on, only to fail later.'

Pippa added water to her own floral arrangements. 'I don't see how I can be expected to take anything in when I'm so tired. I can hardly keep my eyes open.'

'I can cope with the eyes—it's the feet.'

They looked at each other and grinned wryly before flying back to the ward.

'Nurse, pull those curtains back properly round Mr Hills' bed. They're a disgrace.'

'Yes, Sister.'

'And when you've done that you can do the BPs. You do know how?'

'Yes, Sister. We did them in PTS.'

'Fine, well get Nurse Roberts to go along with you just in case. Confidence comes only with experience, and experience comes with time.'

Perhaps I should have those words engraved on my heart or made into a sampler, and keep it over my bed, Pippa thought, as yet another patient submitted docilely to having his blood pressure taken and charted.

'I remember thinking the same thing myself not so long ago,' Anne Roberts consoled. 'The irritating thing is that Sister talks a lot of sense. The only way to learn is by doing things yourself.'

'It's a bit hard on the patients though, isn't it?'

'Not really. We don't do anything drastic without supervision. Mind you, I still squirm when I remember the first injection I ever gave. The poor man nearly hit the roof and wouldn't let me near him again. Not that I could blame him.'

Pippa's brown eyes clouded. 'I'm convinced I'll never be able to do it. It's all very well sticking needles into oranges in PTS. It's not even so bad practising with sterile water on each other. I just don't know how I'll cope with the real thing.'

'When it comes to it you'll be fine. The first is always the worst, but you'll be surprised how nice and sympathetic most patients are. By the way, have you looked through the case notes yet?'

'No. Am I supposed to?'

'It's not compulsory, but it is encouraged. It helps give you an insight into the patients' symptoms and treatments and it helps you to identify the patients more quickly. A word of warning though. Never let Sister hear you refer to anyone as bed number so and so, or she'll have your guts for garters.'

'Thanks for the warning. I'll remember.' Pippa

smiled appreciatively. Not that she would have done it anyway, she thought, as she went to report to Sister. In fact it was surprising how quickly the patients were becoming individuals to her, after that first initial shock of being faced with twenty-six strangers and the dread that she would never remember them, or mix up the medicines.

Sister was speaking on the telephone and beckoned her into the office as she tapped on the door. Pippa stood in front of the desk wondering whether she would ever have enough confidence to accept responsibility for a hectic ward.

'Yes, I realise you're busy, but if you could let me have those results as soon as possible . . .' Sister's face bore the harassed look of one who has gone through the arguments a thousand times before. 'Fine, I'd be grateful.' The phone went down and she turned to Pippa. 'I take it you've finished the BPs?'

'Yes, Sister.'

'Jolly good.' Lisa Carson's face relaxed gradually as she studied the girl in front of her. 'Not so bad, is it, once you get used to it?'

'No, Sister. Actually I quite enjoyed it. Er, I was wondering if I could possibly read through the case notes some time?'

A look of approval met the suggestion. 'Certainly. I'm all for it, provided of course you return them to their proper place in the file. I'm pleased to see you showing signs of initiative.'

'Well, actually, Sister, Nurse Roberts suggested it.'

'Did she? Well she's certainly the right person to give you any hints. It's the little things, like learning to get to know your patient and their symptoms, which can be of enormous help, especially when it comes to writing up your notes.' They headed for the door and she glanced at the clock. 'Fifteen minutes to visiting. Where on earth does the time go?'

Where indeed? Pippa wondered. There were already several faces peering through the ward doors. 'Do I let them in, Sister?'

'Goodness no, not yet.' She saw the look on the girl's face and explained. 'It's not sheer pettiness on my part to keep them waiting. I'm all for visitors, they do an enormous job in boosting morale, but the work of the ward has to be done too. It's important that those patients still confined to bed should be made comfortable, given bedpans if necessary, before we open the doors and everyone comes streaming in. Some of our gentlemen are elderly and become easily upset or embarrassed. As you should know.'

The potent reminder of her fiasco with Mr Tate's bedpan brought a quick shaft of colour to Pippa's face. 'Yes, Sister.'

'Well, it's the same sort of thing we try to avoid whenever possible. Some patients have to have their medication between meals too, which means now.' Sister frowned as she took the medicine trolley keys from her pocket. 'By the way, have you seen Mr Fisher?'

Pippa did a rapid flip through her mental file. Fisher. Slight heart attack, history of severe bronchitis. In his late fifties. 'No, I haven't, Sister, not for some time actually.'

Lisa Carson's lips pursed. 'Honestly, that man. Nurse Gibson . . .' She hailed Pete. 'Have you seen Mr Fisher?'

He looked towards the empty bed space. 'No, Sister. Day room possibly. Hoping we won't notice he's missing when we hand out the pills, I dare say.'

'You're probably right. Could you both go and see if you can track him down please? I sometimes wonder if he thinks he's here for our benefit rather than his own. He shouldn't be wandering too far, anyway.'

'I'll check the day room now.'

'Fine. Nurse, you take the bathroom and kitchen and anywhere else you can think of. And when you find him, remind him it's time for visitors. That may bring him a little more willingly.'

'I wouldn't count on it, Sister,' Pete grinned. 'From what I've seen of his wife, they don't exactly hit it off.'

'Oh dear. Well, find him anyway. He'll have to sort out his own marital problems, but making sure he has his medication is ours.'

Pippa went one way, Pete the other. Liz was just coming from behind the curtains round one of the beds, bedpan in hand.

'You haven't seen Mr Fisher, I suppose?'

'Fisher? Don't think so.'

'Never mind. He can't be far away.' Pippa put her head round the door of the kitchen. It was empty, awaiting the arrival of the tea trolley and the flurry of activity it would cause. The bathroom was just off the ward. It was empty too.

A tiny flutter of alarm made its presence felt, cutting a frown into her brow as her footsteps quickened. Suppose he had had another attack? He could be lying somewhere, helpless, afraid. Her heart thudded as she pushed open the door of the second bathroom, steeling herself for the sight of

Mr Fisher lying on the floor. The anti-climax when she found nothing drew a quivering sigh of relief from her lips as she closed the door again and marched briskly in the direction of the men's toilets, pushing the door and gasping, winded, as it made ominous contact with some obstruction. She heard a low groan and her heart sank.

'Mr Fisher?' Shaking, she eased herself in through the gap and found a figure huddled on the floor in a corner. He seemed to be choking and clutching at his throat. 'Mr Fisher, what is it?' She knelt beside him, took one look at his rolling eyes and odd colour and without hesitation flew, trembling, to plunge her hand on the cardiac arrest button.

Sister Tutor's words came flying back. 'In cases of cardiac arrest, do not hesitate. Summon immediate qualified help, then keep out of the way. All doctors within the immediate vicinity will respond to the call within seconds.'

It worked, too. Somehow she hadn't expected it to be quite so quick. As she flew back to the patient, other figures, mostly in white coats, were already appearing from all directions, looking at her with smiles of sympathy.

'Where is he?'

'In there, on the floor behind the door.' Her voice sounded odd but no one seemed to notice or care.

'Get the oxygen.' She fled to where the wheeled cylinder was kept and raced back with it to where the toilet now resembled something like a rugby scrum. She caught a glimpse of Sister easing her way through the crowd.

'What happened, Nurse?'

It was ridiculous the way her hands were shaking. 'It's Mr Fisher, Sister. I found him on the floor. He seemed to be choking.'

Another figure appeared in the doorway and her heart gave a quite irrational bump of pleasure as Julius Sterling stepped quietly into the fray, taking calm control.

'Someone pressed the cardiac button.'

'Y . . . yes, sir. I did.' The grey eyes narrowed momentarily in her direction, then she was edged aside as still more white coats arrived.

Pete Gibson hovered too. 'Anything I can do, Sister?'

Pippa listened, taking it all in as the great life-saving machine swung effortlessly into motion around her, feeling her throat tighten with pride to think that she was just one tiny part of that team.

'Yes, Nurse. Get Mr Fisher's bed prepared, quickly please. Screens, oxygen, case notes.'

The murmur of voices dwindled and Pippa felt the colour drain from her face as she saw the cardiologist straighten up. They were too late. She felt her throat tighten with regret and remorse that she hadn't found the man sooner, and tears stung at her eyes.

'I don't think that's going to be necessary, Sister.' He seemed to be having difficulty speaking, as if overcome by some intense emotion, and Pippa wondered what it must be like to be faced with the awesome responsibility of trying to save life. She brushed a hand across her wet cheek. Then, suddenly, with horrified fascination, her gaze widened as the white coats drew gradually back, smiling at her with oddly pitying glances. Incredulously her eyes went from the guilt-ridden face of the patient to that other which seemed to be regarding her with chilling, silent mockery.

'M . . . Mr Fisher. But . . . you can't! You're . . .' She saw the nerve pulsing in Julius Sterling's jaw and was vaguely aware of the figures dispersing around her, avoiding her look of stunned confusion. Sister stood with her eyes closed, as if in some private act of meditation.

'I take it you are responsible for this?' Julius Sterling said.

She stared at him, unaware of the look of misery in her eyes. 'But . . . I don't understand. I thought he was having a heart attack.'

For an instant his face contorted in what she thought might be laughter until his mouth tightened grimly. 'As it happens, he wasn't. It seems our Mr Fisher was simply indulging in an illicit cigarette and your own, somewhat abrupt arrival rather took the wind out of his sails.'

'You mean . . . he was smoking? He wasn't ill after all?' Humiliation brought a lump to Pippa's throat which threatened to choke her. She could feel the tears pricking at her eyes as she prayed for the floor to open and swallow her up before the anger could descend.

'Don't you know yet, Nurse, that this is what patients who are denied their cigarettes do?' His voice was surprisingly quiet as he motioned a group of grinning medical students tersely away. 'Mr Fisher knew he wasn't supposed to smoke, but habit dies hard. That's why he was hiding in here. It was a little unfortunate, to say the least, that you happened to barge in, knock the breath out of him and immediately jump to the wrong conclusions.'

'But I . . .' She had to bite her lip to stop it

trembling. 'I don't know what to say.'

'I'd suggest you say nothing at all. You have a lot to learn. I imagine today will have provided a salutory lesson.'

Pippa stared at her shoes, unaware of the white misery in her face. It was true, but how was she ever going to trust herself again, especially in a real emergency?

'I'm sorry. I've been such an idiot.' She brushed the tears away and looked up just in time to see the faint flicker of annoyance in his eyes.

'Nothing is gained by making a drama out of it, Nurse. Everyone makes mistakes.'

Somehow she doubted that he had ever made a mistake in his life. She was never going to live it down. In a ridiculous way it would even have been more bearable if he had really been angry—instead of which he was being understanding and far too nice.

She sniffed hard, and it wasn't until he handed her a large, white hanky that she realised they were alone. Everyone, Sister included, had apparently melted away, presumably to leave her to face the music.

'Here. For heaven's sake, blow your nose and don't cry. It isn't the end of the world, you know.'

Wasn't it? Right now it felt as if it was. Pippa blew hard, held out the hanky and withdrew it quickly, pushing it into her pocket. 'I'll wash it and return it.'

'Don't worry about it.' He sounded vaguely annoyed. But then, he had every right to be, she thought. 'Just . . . just be more careful in future before you press the alarm and plunge the entire hospital into chaos.'

She nodded, too miserable to speak. 'I was so sure he was dying and I panicked.'

'Yes, well, as you can see, apart from a hefty case of embarrassment, no harm's done.' She wasn't sure whether he was referring to herself or Mr Fisher. 'I'd suggest you get your patient back to the ward and, if possible, in future keep a better eye on him. As for you,' he eyed the shame-faced man who had had the grace to hover, 'perhaps you'd give some thought in future to the fact that we make the rules for the patients' benefit, not our own. Nurse has quite enough to do without chasing after you.'

With a curt nod of his head he was gone, leaving Mr Fisher looking very sheepish and Pippa staring after him, open-mouthed with disbelief. He had actually defended her. At least . . . she thought he had.

She escorted Mr Fisher back to the ward, her state of shock equalling his own and tinged by a distinct yet quite indefinable feeling of euphoria. It was short-lived, however, as she returned to the ward and a forthcoming interview with Sister, which was in no way likely to be a pleasant one!

'Never mind, ducks. Don't let it get you down.'

Jim Spiller's proffered advice brought a wavering smile to Pippa's lips as she checked his pulse for the third time. Had anyone cared to check her own, they would have found it decidedly shaky, she thought, and not surprising after her interview with Sister. Not that she had been so much reprimanded as made to feel utterly foolish, and just at this moment she wasn't at all sure which was worse.

'I'm sure you acted out of the best of motives,

again.' There had been a barely perceptible pause before the latter word as Lisa Carson had studied the girl in front of her.

'Oh yes, Sister.'

'Yes, well I know you are taught the correct procedures for an emergency, Nurse, and you reacted with commendable speed. But perhaps in future you should take just sufficient time to think first before causing such wholesale disruption.'

As if I needed telling . . . Pippa bent to the task of stripping and making a bed, her actions automatic, her face troubled and flushed with annoyance. She smoothed the bedspread and neatened the edges, sighing as she straightened up. It was no good. She had to snap out of it. But it wasn't so easy when the memory of the enigmatic expression on Julius Sterling's handsome face flashed briefly into her mind as she marched down the ward and into the kitchen to begin energetically stacking cups and saucers on to the trolley.

She was engrossed in ladling jam into a dish when Pete poked his head round the door.

'Er, I hate to say it, but there's a pretty restless crowd of visitors outside threatening to beat down the door. Hadn't you better let them in before something nasty happens?'

Pippa gasped as her gaze flew to the clock. 'Oh no. I'd forgotten all about them.' Shedding her plastic apron, she fled past him to fling open the swing doors, only just managing to step back in time as the hordes descended.

'It's like being trampled by a herd of raging elephants,' she complained to Liz later as they handed out teas and bread and butter and jam. 'Cake, Mr Thomas? No, I'm afraid it's walnut.'

'But I only like fruit and cherry, Nurse.'

She summoned a smile, wishing her own problems were so easily settled. 'Well, perhaps tomorrow. How about a biscuit then?'

'Any ginger nuts?'

'Er, no.' She examined the plate and shook her head. 'Sorry. How about a nice digestive?'

'I'll just have the tea and bread and butter.' Clearly unimpressed, Mr Thomas retreated with his cup behind his newspaper and Pippa moved the trolley to the next bed.

'Poor chap. I haven't seen him have any visitors yet. I expect he's lonely.'

'I doubt it.' Liz spooned jam on to a plate. 'He told me this morning he'd rather not be pestered. He's in for ten days and intends making the most of it.'

'In that case I hope he gets his fruit cake tomorrow, or life won't be worth living.'

The visitors trundled out in dribs and drabs, leaving flowers to be arranged, bowls for fruit and eggs to be marked with individual patient's names. Medicines followed, the routine TPRs, and then an emergency perforated ulcer had to be admitted, stepping up the tempo again.

Half an hour after the time she should officially have gone off duty, Pippa finally heard herself dismissed.

'All right, Nurse. You can go off now. Just drop this file in at Records on the way, will you, and don't be late in tomorrow. Aren't you in Study Block for the afternoon?'

'Yes, Sister.'

'Best of luck then.'

As if she knows I'll jolly well need it, Pippa

thought, as she made her way to the cloakroom to collect her coat.

The swing doors opened just as she reached them and she stood back, a friendly smile instinctively lightening her face, allowing a tall figure to pass. It wasn't until she met Julius Sterling's gaze that she realised who it was and opened her mouth ready to blurt out yet another apology, but his eyes slid over her with cool indifference before he nodded curtly and walked away, leaving her with the distinct impression that she was the last person he had wanted to see.

It was silly to allow the incident to affect her, she knew, and yet it did. She didn't want to be on unfriendly terms with the consultant, but it seemed there were barriers and he had already clearly defined that she should be on one side and himself on the other. Which was probably by far the safest arrangement, she conceded, sighing heavily as she walked out into the fresh air, carrying just a waft of his elusive aftershave with her.

CHAPTER FIVE

'I HAVE READ your essays.' Sister Tutor gazed at the row of attentive faces in front of her with an air of pained disappointment. 'I can't say I was impressed. In fact what came over most clearly was an impression that most of you were more concerned with filling ten pages than with any noticeable regard for the quality of the work you were handing in.' She moved to stand in front of the desk. 'I can only assume you imagined I would be sufficiently impressed by the quantity and that I wouldn't pay any attention to the quality, in which case you were sadly mistaken.'

By now any smiles had vanished and the occupant of each uncomfortable chair was sitting bolt upright. She reached for the pile of papers and tossed them on to the nearest table as if it were a wastepaper basket.

'You will find your marks correspond to the scale of your own enthusiasm. One thing you will understand before you leave here at the end of this afternoon. I am not prepared to put up with anything less than your best. If you feel too much is being asked of you then the remedy lies in your own hands. No one is forcing you to become nurses. The choice is yours, but I will repeat what I have said on many occasions; that if you wish to gain qualifications at this hospital, you will abide by its standards or you will cease to waste our time.'

She paused, smiling into a nervous silence. 'I was

also under the impression that there were a number of male nurses in this group.' The guilty six squirmed sheepishly in uncomfortable anticipation. 'In future gentlemen, I want to see you integrating with your fellow students, taking an active part in all aspects of your training. This is not some elite gentlemen's club. You are here to become nurses, and merely because you are men does not exclude you from certain sections of the training. I shall look to see a marked change in attitude. Right, and now that we understand one another, I'm sure we shall all feel more relaxed.'

Twenty rigid white faces seemed to indicate some doubt, but Sister Tutor either was, or chose to be, oblivious to it. A paper was deposited on each desk, face down. Everyone stared at it as if in some desperate hope that they might be able to read the print through it and get a head start.

'Very well, you have two hours. Write legibly, answer those questions you know first. You can always go back to any you have doubts about. Right . . . begin.'

For the next two hours the room was silent except for the scratching of pens and an occasional cough. At the ninety-minute stage Sister quietly announced the time, and Pippa threw a panic-stricken glance at the other industriously lowered heads around her. She wasn't going to make it. Her mind had gone a total blank and there were still two questions left.

She ran through the first and heaved a sigh of cautious relief as she chewed at the pen and began to write. Ten minutes left. Her flushed gaze rose to catch Sister's eye, and for one moment she had the crazy notion that Sister's lips had actually smiled reassuringly. It was a mistake of course. She lowered her head and read again, hearing her own slight gasp of incredulity at the words. 'Describe the layout of a sterile trolley and the procedure for cleansing a post-operative wound.' She looked up again. Sister was staring out of the window, her face expressionless. Imagination could play very funny tricks.

Just as 'time-up' was called, Pippa wrote the last word and put her pen down to find herself shaking with delayed reaction.

Well, if she failed now, that was it. She wouldn't be allowed to stay even if she wanted to, and suddenly she did want to, very much, in spite of Mr Julius Sterling.

They filed out into the corridor and began to head, as if by a common need, towards the junior coffee lounge. For once the customary idle chatter was missing. Even Liz looked subdued as she caught up with Pippa.

'How did it go?'

'I feel sick. I spent the first fifteen minutes chewing the top off my pen and just staring at the paper, hoping it would eventually start to make sense.'

They joined the queue for coffees and carried them to a corner table. 'It wasn't really quite as bad as I expected, not once I'd got past the initial shock.' Liz heaped sugar into her cup. 'At least I managed to do the one on sterile procedure. Do you think Sister Tutor included it on purpose?'

'I should think it's highly unlikely. I think the whole paper was designed to inflict the maximum degree of torture, and judging by my efforts today, there's no way I'll ever pass my finals. Even supposing I ever get that far.'

'Oh, come on. Did you answer all the questions?'

'More or less. I waffled a bit on the second, vitamins and their values. Sister's bound to notice. She has eyes like a hawk.'

'Well, she'll notice mine too then, not that there's a thing we can do about it now, so I don't know why we're sitting here worrying.'

'I suppose because it's really only just hit me that I could be out of here and looking for another job in a couple of weeks' time if I don't get through. We're not assessed only on this paper, anyway. Our general progress through PTS is taken into account as well, when they decide if we're to be allowed to stay or not.' She gulped at her coffee, trying not to think of the awful ignominy of having to hand back uniforms and books and saying goodbye to the group who had begun as strangers and had already become friends. She sniffed hard. 'I think I must be getting a cold.'

'It must be catching,' Liz said heavily. 'Judging by the number of hankies in evidence.'

Morning came, bringing with it an aching head and hollow eyes. None of which escaped Staff Nurse Baker's eagle-keen gaze as they trooped into the office for report next day.

Wedging herself at the back nearest to the door, and standing strategically behind Pete Gibson, Pippa muttered, 'I'd forgotten it was Sister's day off. That's all I need.'

'Nurse Benedict, if you have quite finished, may we begin? We have a long day ahead of us and I would like to get on.'

Pippa squirmed. 'Yes, Staff. Sorry, Staff.'

'I'm glad to hear it, and tidy your cap, Nurse. It's a disgrace.'

Pippa stifled a groan. It was clear from the stormy glint in Staff's eye that she had been ear-marked as a trouble-maker and from now on every move she made was going to come under close scrutiny.

Pete Gibson moved slightly, whether inten-tionally or not, cutting her off from Staff's gaze, and Pippa felt like kissing him from sheer relief as they progressed with slow thoroughness through the report before they were all allowed to file out on to the ward to perform their allotted tasks.

It had been a relatively quiet night. One admis-sion. The patient had had a heart attack three days previously and had developed a blood clot in his leg. He had undergone emergency surgery and was back on the ward where he would be watched and checked carefully at regular intervals. Two new patients were due in for routine ops the following day and three were being discharged.

'And so it goes on,' Liz murmured as they were dismissed. 'Like some huge great conveyor belt.'

There wasn't time to chat as they went their separate ways, but she caught Pete's broad wink and blushed before ducking into the kitchen to collect hot water and a cloth to clean the lockers. She sighed at the thought that the punishing itinerary set out before them in PTS seemed de-signed for the sole purpose of ensuring that no one had either the time or the energy even for an idle contemplation of any extra-curricular activities.

Lockers duly swabbed to Staff Nurse Baker's grudging satisfaction, she was despatched to morn-ing coffee and returned to help give out the patients' mid-morning drinks. At ten-thirty pre-cisely the ward doors swung open and her heart gave a simultaneous lurch as Julius Sterling strode in, surrounded by an entourage of goggle-eyed medical students.

Pippa's hands suddenly became clamped on the jug of orange squash she was holding. He was coming towards her and she felt the waves of alternate hot and cold sweeping over her as she debated whether she should carry it to its intended locker at the bed where he was now standing, or make a bid for escape. The jug and the situation were removed from her hands as Staff appeared and briskly ordered her to, 'Count the linen, please, Nurse.'

It was as near to being banished in total disgrace as it was possible to come, she knew, as she dragged herself away to spend the next half-hour resentfully counting and recounting sheets and pillowcases in the tiny linen cupboard which boasted the mocking title of room. Someone undoubtedly had a sense of humour, but she wasn't in any mood to share it and her eyes sparked with the determination to say so as the door opened at last, offering freedom.

She turned and froze, her mouth clamped into a trembling line, as Julius Sterling lounged non-chalantly in the doorway, eyeing her with the kind of sardonic amusement which brought the colour surging to her cheeks.

'Good morning, Nurse. Enjoying your work?'

Enjoying it? At this precise moment she hated it almost as much as she hated him. She choked on a response as he thrust a paper into her hand.

'Perhaps you'll see that Staff gets that list, will you? She was gone before I remembered it.'

'Yes, of course, sir.'

She waited for him to go, but he stood there, gazing steadily at her as if trying to memorise every detail of her face until she fidgeted uncomfortably. 'Was there anything else, sir?' She felt like adding, 'Are my eyes the wrong colour? Is my mouth too large?' Instead she said, 'I have to get back to the ward if you've finished your round.'

She caught what might have been just the faintest suggestion of laughter in his eyes. 'Oh dear. In disgrace again, are we? What is it this time?'

'Not at all.' She turned away, furiously, before he could see the colour spilling into her face. The only cause of any trouble in her life was standing right in front of her now, making her extremely nervous as she began indiscriminately stacking and re-stacking bundles of sheets. If she ignored him he was bound to go away. The linen cupboard was far too small for them both. Even smaller when one of the sheets fell to land at his feet and he bent to retrieve it, coming even closer as he returned it to her shaking hands.

He frowned. 'Are you always this nervous, or is it just me? I don't bite, you know.'

Pippa stared into the dark, dangerous pool of his eyes and thought, *he simply has no idea*. She closed her eyes again, shutting out the very foolish temptation to reach up and brush the hair from his face, and drew in a quivering breath of surprise as his lips suddenly brushed gently against her mouth. She felt incapable of movement, even if she had wanted to move—and she didn't. The pressure of his mouth had been so light against her own, and yet she had to take a deep breath to keep control of her emotions. He saw the sudden fading of her colour and frowned, mistaking it.

'Am I really such an ogre?'

She looked at him, her eyes widening with confusion, wondering what she had done to provoke the sudden tension she saw in his face.

'Y . . . You shouldn't be in here. Sister may come in.'

For an instant the heavy brows drew together and she sensed, irrationally, that he was angry as he stepped back. 'You're probably right. I shouldn't, not if I had any sense.'

In spite of herself, she laughed at the notion that he could be afraid of Sister. 'I shouldn't think there's any danger of you getting a telling off. That's a privilege strictly reserved for the likes of student nurses.' Pippa's voice faded as his fingers suddenly took her chin, turning it up to his as he kissed her mouth again very softly, feeling her lips tremble before he broke away saying quietly, 'That wasn't quite what I had in mind.'

Then what *had* he had in mind? She felt herself released and left to battle with a shock of emotions, none of which made sense, except that she had wanted the experience to go on, last for ever. It didn't, of course. Dreams never did, especially when they concerned men like Julius Sterling.

She pressed her hands shakily to her burning face, wondering why. Why had he kissed her? Why had he stopped?

He seemed about to say something, then apparently changed his mind as he muttered a soft oath and turned and left, leaving her standing there, paper in hand, heart performing a crazy little dance. It was some seconds before she realised he had gone and she came back to reality, blinking hard. It was pretty obvious, when she thought about it, why he had stopped. Wasn't he, after all, the senior consultant and she a student nurse? There was one thing to be said for barriers, they made a safe place to retreat to when things began to get involved.

She gulped hard on the uncomfortable tightness in her throat. Enjoying her work? What chance was there of her ever doing that when he seemed to be doing everything he could to make it impossible?

'Nurse Benedict?'

She spun round. 'Yes, Staff?'

'Go to lunch now please. I want you back on the ward in one hour promptly.'

'Yes, Staff.' Pippa went in search of Liz and found her in the sluice. 'I've been ordered to go to lunch. Are you coming?'

Liz glanced up sufficiently to show eyes reddened from weeping, and Pippa closed the door quickly behind her. 'What's the matter? Not Baker, is it?'

Liz's mouth compressed. 'Honestly, that woman! I don't believe she has an ounce of humanity in her entire body.'

'Why, what's happened?'

'You name it, I've apparently done it—all wrong, according to Staff. She had me stripping and re-making a bed three times before she was satisfied, and then I was blamed for the sluice being what she called a disgrace. Hence the reason I'm here now, with orders to clean it until Staff can see her face in every surface.'

'I wonder she wants to bother.' Pippa made a glum attempt at humour and was relieved to see a smile flicker, if only briefly, on Liz's face.

'It wasn't my fault, anyway. The new orderly was

in here before me and I'm sure she was having a crafty smoke. I haven't the heart to shop her, but one of these days she'll get caught. Anyway, I was nearest to hand so I got the blame, and you know Baker. You answer back on pain of death or instant dismissal. Not that I'm all that convinced right now that I wouldn't almost prefer it.'

They shared a moment's mutual sympathetic silence. 'So you're not coming to lunch, I take it?'

'Ha! No way I'm afraid. I'll have to take second, and by the time I finish here I'll be lucky if I have time for a sandwich, which no doubt will be crisp and curling round the edges with my present luck. Perhaps you could save me a biscuit.'

Liz went back to her polishing and Pippa made her way downstairs, not looking forward to a solitary meal in the crowded cafeteria, where there didn't seem to be one friendly face among the chattering groups.

Having queued at the counter she carried her tray with its plate of shepherd's pie to a corner table, ate half-heartedly and, dismissing the idea of going back to the ward early, decided to spend the half-hour that was left, sitting in the garden with a newspaper.

There was a nicely secluded corner, tucked away between the maternity block and Outpatients, scarcely used except by the occasional mum-in-waiting, sometimes to be seen strolling heavily backwards and forwards in the hope that activity might help things along. Obviously at this moment the mothers were all producing without assistance, and she breathed a sigh of relief at finding the bench empty.

Newspaper at the ready, open at the crossword,

she filled in the first clue lethargically and sat back, closing her eyes. Twenty blissful minutes before she need throw herself back into Staff Nurse Baker's clutches. The sun was warm. The first few leaves had started to fall from the trees. It was nice to smell roses instead of antiseptic.

Her eyes flickered open again. 'Three down . . .' She really wasn't giving this the attention it deserved.

'How about sex?' A voice demanded laughingly from behind her, sending her jolting forward as a pair of hands came over her eyes.

'Pete Gibson, how dare you?' Hot with confusion, she leapt to retrieve the scattered paper, hardly daring to look at the quiet laughter in his eyes.

'My dear girl, I was referring to the crossword. The female gender.' He tutted. 'Just what did you think I had in mind?'

She snatched the pages furiously from his shaking grasp, knowing perfectly well what he had in mind. 'Thank you very much. I already had it.'

'Oh, really? Lucky you.'

'The answer, I mean.' She gritted her teeth, not knowing whether to laugh or hit him. 'You're deliberately misunderstanding.'

'Ah, a burden we both suffer in that case. I'm frequently misunderstood.'

'Somehow I doubt that.' She gathered the paper and the shreds of her dignity together. 'Anyway, I have to get back, so you can have this if you like. Since you're such an expert.'

'Sweetest, I've never said that.'

'Haven't you? Then it must have been implied.'

He was smilingly, teasingly close, and curiosity

rather than any other emotion prompted her not to
avoid the kiss he planted on her lips. It was nice.
Not exactly earth-shattering, but something she
could probably quite get to like. Along with at
least a dozen or so other females. The thought
made her back away, wondering what suddenly
made her feel that with the right man it could be
very different. She shrugged the idea aside, along
with a tantalisingly brief image of a pair of dark
eyes which somehow, frustratingly, bore no resemblance to Pete's. She smiled shakily.

'I don't quite know how we got on to this particular subject, but it's time I was back on the ward.'

'I'll come with you.' He fell into step beside her
and she squashed the comment that she would
rather go alone than face Staff's disapproval when
they put in an appearance together. Staff dis-
approved strongly of fraternisation between members of staff, even if it didn't exist except in her own
head!

CHAPTER SIX

'I STILL can't believe it.' Pippa joined the mass drift of her fellow students towards the PTS coffee room where they queued and carried their cups to sit at tables in various stunned little groups. 'We made it. Perhaps I ought to go and take another look at the notice-board, just in case there's a mistake.'

'There isn't,' Liz said affably. 'I double-checked for both of us.' The general air of smug satisfaction was brief but glorious. It lasted until Sister Tutor walked in, the inevitable list in her hand and an attitude which reminded them sharply that this was only the beginning. There was far worse to come.

'First of all, let me offer my congratulations to those of you who passed.' As if by some silent agreement no one looked at the three empty places. Everyone knew that Cynthia Hopper had chickened out at the last minute, deciding to leave even before attempting the exams. It wasn't that she couldn't do the work, more that she had felt demeaned in some way by the tasks she had been called upon to do. As if there was some nasty smell under her nose.

'Let's face it, it's something you've jolly well got to get used to,' had been the general verdict when such things had been discussed over the many previous coffees. So no one had been exactly surprised when 'La Cynthia' had packed her bags and left, following a long and serious chat with Sister.

'Who else is out?' Liz whispered.

Pippa scanned the group. 'Maggie Crofts isn't here, but that could be coincidence, I suppose.'

'I doubt it. I passed her on the stairs, looking very red-eyed.'

A sudden awareness that it might so easily have been her own name missing from that list, and what it would have meant, sent a shiver of sympathy down Pippa's spine. 'But she could probably try again if she has a word with Sister. After all, it's not as if it was State Finals or anything as important as that.'

'It's still important. We all knew what was at stake.'

'But she tried so hard. She so desperately wanted to nurse.' Pippa subsided beneath Sister's look into a depression which almost, but not quite, managed to take the joy out of her own pass. The fact that it had all probably been sheer luck only added to the twinges of guilt. If that last question had been on anything except sterile procedures . . .

'I'm pleased to be able to say that the standard was generally higher than I had at first expected. Nurse Yeo got the highest grades. Individual marks haven't been published on the list.'

'Probably in order to save us embarrassment,' Pippa whispered.

'But these will be shown on your papers, which I shall return to you this afternoon when each of you come along to my office in turn. For now I simply want to tell you which wards you have been allotted to for your first three months. Some of you will remain where you are.'

'Please God, let me be moved from Men's Surgical.'

'The rest of you have to go where we can fit you in, I'm afraid. Nurses Patterson and Fox to Casualty please. Nurses Greaves and Hansford to Outpatients. Nurses Foster and Dixon to Female Medical. The rest of you stay where you were. Right, I think that's all for now. I'll be pleased to go into any details before you leave. Oh yes, and you will all take a long weekend's leave before beginning your new duties. This is in order to give you time to gather your uniforms and generally prepare for the real business of becoming nurses. Contrary to what many of you may think, you haven't learned it all during the past three months. You are not yet nurses. Only the next three years can turn you into anything remotely resembling the kind of nurse we would welcome here, so from now on it's up to you. Drink up now. Collect your books. Kindly return any borrowed textbooks to the hospital librarian who will not be happy if she has to chase culprits from ward to ward for the next six weeks. Remember, other students need the library facilities too.'

There was something strangely depressing about the speech. 'It's like leaving school all over again,' Pippa bemoaned the fact to Liz as they trotted back to the study block. 'I hated it while I was there, but the minute it was time to leave I suddenly realised it hadn't been quite so bad after all.' She sighed, holding the door open before they ran up the stairs.

'I suppose in a way it is the same. I sometimes find it hard to imagine I'll ever be a real nurse, taking responsibility, making decisions. Don't you think it's all a bit frightening? Perhaps we'll end up like Staff Baker.'

They both looked at each other in silent horror, then burst into a fit of giggles. 'God forbid!'

Sister's approaching footsteps sent them scuttling to collect bags and capes. 'Come along, Nurses. Why are you still here?'

'Sorry, Sister, I left my things.'

'One of these days, Nurse Benedict, you'll forget something far more vital. I can only hope for everyone's sake that you buck up your ideas before you get to Theatre or I dread to think what might happen. Off you go now, both of you. Get some lunch and don't forget to see me this afternoon about your weekend leave.'

'Yes, Sister. Sorry, Sister. Honestly,' she muttered as they ran down the stairs again, 'those words seem to rule my life. 'Yes, Sister, sorry, sister.'

'Never mind. Just remind yourself that one day it will be some frightened little student saying it to you.'

'It doesn't help. I shall know exactly how she feels and I shall sympathise.'

'Oh, come on. You're impossible! Let's get to the dining-room before the rush starts. I'm ravenous.'

They edged into a table and prepared to enjoy the special dispensation of a free afternoon. 'Just think, we won't be sitting in the PTS coffee-lounge again, or seeing the same faces every day.' Pippa stared at Liz. 'We won't be on the same ward. I must be an idiot. It just hadn't occurred to me we'd be split up.'

'Nor to me. Still, I suppose it had to happen some time.'

'Well I wish it was me who was moving. I've

already had it up to here with Staff Nurse Baker and Mr Julius Sterling. Between the two of them I shall be a nervous wreck.'

'I can't say I particularly fancy Women's Med, but we've all got to start somewhere. What really fills me with terror is the thought of working in Theatre. I don't know if I'll be able to cope with it.'

Pippa pushed a heap of Brussels sprouts round her plate. 'Funny. That doesn't bother me at all. Well not now, anyway, and I suppose by the time we actually come to it we shall be more experienced anyway, so it won't be quite the same.'

'I wouldn't mind a stint in Casualty or even Outpatients. In fact I half-hoped my name would come up. Some folk have all the luck.'

'You're not serious, are you?'

'Yes, of course. Why not?'

Pippa shrugged. 'Oh, I don't know. Just that I never think of Cas as part of all this, somehow.' She pushed her plate aside in favour of a dish of trifle topped by a dubious layer of something re-motely resembling cream. 'What are you going to do with your weekend?'

'Haven't a clue. I didn't give it much thought. Well, there didn't seem much point until we knew whether we'd be staying or not.'

Pippa stared, spoon half-way to her mouth. 'You're joking! There was never any doubt about you passing.'

Liz laughed. 'Nothing is that certain. Still, I'll probably stay on here. I'll give my room a clean and sort my uniforms out.'

Pippa abandoned the trifle and sat back. 'I thought I might go to see Emma. I had a letter last week asking me to go over. I expect she wants to show off the twins.'

'Haven't you seen them yet?'

'Oh yes, after they were born, but they were just little blobs then, all shawls and bonnets and they slept all the time. Of course, Emma thought they were the best thing since sliced bread. I hadn't the heart to say I thought it was all a bit boring.'

'I should hope not indeed! Just wait till it's your own squalling little bundle. You'll be unbearable. I can just see you now.'

Pippa stared reflectively into the thickening layer on top of her coffee and wondered why she couldn't see it too. Of course, she had always assumed she would get married some day, when Mr Right came along. She screwed up her eyes, trying to conjure him up, and found herself shocked by an image of a face which had no business being in her thoughts at all.

'I say, are you all right?'

She blinked. 'What? Oh yes. Touch of heartburn or something.' She winced at her own choice of words.

'Hm. I'm not surprised. That steak and kidney pudding is enough to give anyone indigestion. Why not take something for it?'

The question was, Pippa thought miserably, what exactly did one take to ease the kind of ache which seemed to be troubling her at the moment? She shook the thought off. It was probably end-of-PTS nerves. A weekend away would soon put things right.

'How's that brother-in-law of yours by the way?'

'Who, Garrard?' She smiled as they retraced

their steps down the stairs and out into the sunshine. 'Gorgeous.'

'Some people have all the luck.'

'Don't they just?'

CHAPTER SEVEN

SHE HANDED her ticket to the collector and moved with the rest of the crowd towards the exit barrier. Ten yards from it she saw her brother-in-law's familiar tall figure wave before he swooped to gather her and her small suitcase up in his arms and kiss her soundly on the cheek.

'Garrard. It's lovely to see you again. And you're so tanned!'

'It's all this sea air. You should come down more often and take advantage.'

'Oh, if only I could.'

Set breathlessly back on her feet, Pippa recovered her composure, still conscious of a feeling of shyness as she looked up at her sister's husband. It still took some getting used to, the fact that Emma had actually married a senior registrar, and such a good-looking one too. She followed as he led her out to the car and loaded her suitcase into the boot. She was settled into the luxurious upholstery of the passenger seat as he climbed in beside her and turned to smile in her direction.

'Sorry I was late. Emma had intended coming to meet you herself, but we had a slight last-minute crisis so I flew to the rescue instead.'

'Oh, you weren't on duty?' For the first time she took in his dark, formal suit.

'That's okay.' The craggy features creased into a smile. 'My clinic isn't until two-thirty. I've plenty of time to drop you off, but I'm afraid I won't be able to stay and gossip, much as I'd like to. Not that I think it will matter. I'm sure you and Emma will have enough to keep you going all weekend.'

'I expect so.' She smiled, settling back comfortably as he eased the car expertly through the traffic, and thought that it was difficult to associate Garrard with the kind of senior medical staff who could make her life such a misery at Clem's. He seemed so human, unlike some she could mention.

Without being aware of it she sighed, and he caught the sound.

'You're looking a bit peaky. Not working you too hard, are they?'

She pulled a face. 'Not really. I was just thinking, a whole weekend without Sister breathing down my neck. It's a glorious thought.'

'How did the exams go?' He took his gaze briefly from the road.

'Well, I got through. Probably more by luck than judgment, and I don't mind telling you it was probably to Sister Tutor's surprise as much as my own.'

'That bad, was it?' He laughed and the sleek black car purred its way along the coast road, giving occasional glimpses of the blue bays and sandy beaches. 'Well, it's nice to see you again. Emma's been talking about it for ages and dusting and baking.' He seemed to be smiling through narrowed eyes. 'It took her a while to get the hang of making cakes. The first few attempts were a bit like unleavened bread, but she's gradually turning into quite an expert.'

'That sounds like Emma.' It was lovely to relax in the warm sunshine, to breathe in real air instead of antiseptic. Pippa looked at him and frowned. 'What crisis?'

'Hm?'

'You said there had been a last-minute crisis. Not something serious? Emma's not ill or anything like that?'

'Well, not Emma exactly. It's the twins. I'm afraid they've both gone down with a dose of measles. You really have to congratulate the pair of them on their timing, and of course they do everything together.'

'Oh no.'

He grinned. 'It's not so bad. Katy's the worst. Covered from head to toe, poor little thing. David is what you could call more interestingly pink, and they both have runny noses. We did think perhaps we ought to try and warn you, but Emma thought you'd had measles anyway and it was a bit late. The spots didn't appear until this morning.'

Pippa thought hard. 'She's probably right. I seemed to get most things when I was small. Not to worry, anyway. I'm hardly likely to get it at my age and I'd have hated to have to cancel. It's ages since I saw you all. The twins were tiny.'

'Well I warn you, they're now a strapping nine months, cutting teeth, extremely fractious, and Emma will probably weep all over you. She's not had a very easy time of it lately and I'm not around enough to be much help. From a purely selfish point of view you couldn't have come at a better time.' He looked at her and smiled. 'Not that you aren't very welcome any time, you know that. Ah, home at last.' The car slid on to a gravel drive and came to a halt just as a door at the front of the house opened and a familiar figure emerged carrying one pink-cheeked infant on her hip.

'Pippa!'

'Emma!'

They flew into each others arms, embracing over a mop of tiny blond curls as David Blair sucked a thumb and stared in wide-eyed confusion. Garrard unloaded the suitcase, sweeping it and them into the house where the phone was ringing insistently.

'You've grown. How on earth did you manage that? What's it like at Clem's? Tell me who's still there. Have you seen Lisa Carson?'

'Yes, she's a Sister now. On my ward.'

'No!' Squeals of delight. 'Which one?'

'Men's Surgical.'

'Oh, poor you. That's where I fell foul of Sister Meredith. But she was a dear really.'

'She came to the last prize-giving. She asked after you and I told her about the babies, so she sent her love.'

'She did? Fancy her remembering,' Emma said in surprise.

'That's what I thought, but she said there were some you never forget. I didn't have a chance to ask what she meant. And what do you mean, I've grown? It's these shoes. I knew the minute I bought them they were a mistake.' Pippa hopped on one delicately-heeled shoe and grimaced.

David began to howl and the phone continued to ring until Garrard lunged towards it, gesturing the pair of them into the kitchen. 'Blair speaking. Yes. Right. Fine, I can be with you in half an hour.' He replaced the receiver and kissed his wife and son and Pippa in turn. 'Sorry, I've got to leave you. An emergency just came in and they want me to take a look. Not that I think I shall be missed here.' He was already reaching for his briefcase. 'Don't talk yourselves hoarse before I get home this evening, will you? I'm afraid I've no idea what time I'll be back. You know what the clinics are like.'

'I should by now.' Emma smilingly eased her son on to her other hip and watched her husband rush out of the house. 'Come on, let's have some coffee. I'll feed the babies and you can tell me everything. I must have years of catching up to do.'

'Where's Katy?' Pippa asked.

'In her cot, poor little sausage. She was awake most of last night and she's absolutely exhausted today. To be perfectly honest, it's quite a relief to have half an hour of relative peace.'

'Here, let me hold David.' Pippa took the baby on her knee, letting his exploring, chubby little fingers roam over her face as she watched her sister. 'You look a bit whacked yourself.'

'Well, the twins are a bit of handful right now, but you can hardly blame them, and I keep telling myself it can only get better.'

Pippa smiled. 'Being married obviously suits you. Garrard too.'

'Yes, doesn't it?' Emma heaped coffee into cups and poured on water, adding milk as she smiled reflectively. 'It's funny now to think I used to be so scared of him. I mean, I was a student and he was senior registrar and every time we met the most diabolical things seemed to happen.' Her expression became wistful. 'I can't imagine why he ever married me.'

'Can't you?' Pippa smiled and felt oddly sad. 'I'd say he's head over heels with you and his babies. You're jolly lucky. You should meet our new consultant.'

'Stuffy, is he?'

'Stuffy? I wouldn't say that exactly.' No, there was definitely nothing even remotely stuffy about Julius Sterling, she thought, ignoring a frustratingly vivid picture of the provocative mouth. 'He's just not the sort I get on very well with. We don't exactly see eye to eye. Not that I'm saying he isn't perfectly reasonable.' Except when he's kissing me, the thought invaded.

Emma tore her gaze from her son. 'I gather you don't like him.'

'I really don't know him that well.' Pippa sipped her coffee, letting the atmosphere of peace gradually waft over her.

'I don't suppose Clem's has changed much, has it?'

'Not really. I seem to spend most of my time either dodging Staff Nurse Baker or keeping out of the way every time someone above the status of medical student walks on to the ward.'

'You're right. It hasn't changed.' Emma tucked a strand of hair behind her ear and gazed into the space above her coffee-cup.

'Do you miss it?'

'Good heavens no! I don't have time, not right now, anyway.'

'Will you ever go back?'

'I don't know. I feel guilty about the waste. I mean, I did the first part of my training, then left to marry Garrard. We've talked about it, but I think I'd be more likely to find a job as a medical receptionist if the time ever came when I felt I needed to work. But I can't imagine it, and to be honest, Garrard's work keeps me fairly busy, what with the entertaining and so on.'

Pippa held a brick out for her nephew. 'You've changed.'

'Settled down, you mean. Well, that's Garrard's influence. Not that life is without its little ups and downs, mind you. Like tonight, for instance. I'd better make a start on getting myself organised or we won't be able to eat. Unless we whisk the twins into the Mini and rush down to the shops.'

'Why don't we, after lunch?'

'Why not? The fresh air will probably do them good. Usually I have Mrs Rogers in to help, but her husband is sick so I'm coping—but I do miss her.'

'I seem to have picked the worst possible time to come.'

'Oh no. The very best! I've been longing to see you. I needed a familiar, unspotty face right now.'

They drank their coffee and munched biscuits in companionable silence. St Clement's seemed a million miles away and it was best not to think that freedom only lasted for one weekend.

Emma yawned. 'Sorry. We seem to have had a few bad nights lately. I hope you've brought your ear plugs with you, you're probably going to need them.'

'Don't worry. I've got used to falling asleep the minute my head touches the pillow. Tell you what though, write me a list of what you need from the shops. Point me in the right direction and I'll get whatever you want. I'll enjoy the walk, in fact I'd welcome it. Life seems to have revolved totally around the hospital lately. I'm almost getting to the stage where I feel out of place unless I'm walking down a corridor.'

'Are you sure you wouldn't mind?' Emma leapt

at the idea. 'I really don't feel I should take the babies out.'

'I'd love to. Why don't you put your feet up?' Pippa suggested.

'What a nice idea. You should definitely come more often.'

A shrill wail brought the coffee-break to an abrupt end. 'That's Katy. Come on, you take one, I'll take the other. You couldn't arrange to stay on a permanent basis, I suppose?'

'Wish I could!' Pippa chuckled as they trotted upstairs together. It was like being in another world, peaceful, domesticated, rather nice. The sort of life, she thought rather wistfully, that she would be quite happy to settle for.

The bedroom was light and airy with coloured mobiles hanging from the ceiling and pictures dotting the walls. Leaning over the cot Pippa experienced a sense of shock at the tiny but perfect replica of her sister who smiled, red-cheeked, and held up a chubby hand.

'Hello, Spotty,' Emma cooed.

'Now is that any way to talk to my favourite niece?'

Emma reached down to lift the carroty-haired infant and pulled a face. 'Phew, Katy Blair, what have you done? I think I'd better deal with this little matter of rising damp, then we can all have lunch. Come on, poppet.' Katy rubbed at her nose and buried her spotty face against her mother's shoulder. 'She'll feel more sociable when I've changed her.'

'Aren't you lucky, having a doctor in the family to cope with these little emergencies. It must be marvellous.'

'What, Garrard? You must be joking! He gets into the most awful panic if one of them as much as sneezes twice. You wouldn't think it, would you? I mean, he's usually so strong and dependable. You never know with men, do you?'

'You don't indeed,' Pippa thought, and decided they were an enigma she would rather not try to fathom. This was one weekend when she was going to relax and enjoy herself and nothing, but nothing, was going to be allowed to spoil it.

With lunch over and cleared away, the twins, who were both hot and fractious, went for an afternoon nap and Pippa heaved herself mentally out of the state of lethargy which seemed to be enveloping her. 'If you've got that list ready, I'll go to the shops before I fall asleep.'

'Take the Mini if you like,' Emma offered.

'No thanks. The walk will do me good.' She stretched and yawned. 'It's so beautiful around here. How come you aren't surrounded by tourists?'

'Oh, they tend mostly to head for the bigger resorts along the coast. We're lucky here, tucked away in this little bay. Strangers don't usually even know it exists, so they don't bother us. It's nice. If you came more often you might get to know it.'

'I'd like to, but you know how it is, especially once we start on the wards in earnest.'

Emma gave a slightly sideways look at the pale features and vague shadows which made her sister's eyes look like smudges of brown velvet. 'You look pretty tired yourself.'

'I'm just not used to it, that's all. They say after a while you don't even notice the aches and pains, but I'm still waiting for it to happen. PTS was a bit

hectic. There were times when none of us thought
we'd get through.'

'Well, perhaps things will ease up now.'

Pippa stared out of the window, watching the
distant sea changing from silver-blue to grey. Its
unpredictability reminded her uncomfortably of
Julius Sterling and she pushed the thought away.
'I'd better get going if you want these things. I'll be
as quick as I can.'

'That's okay. I expect Garrard when I see him. It
depends on how the clinic goes. Sometimes it's
straightforward, other times he gets caught up. I
often wonder if he has any sense of time at all.'

Pippa reached for the shopping basket and battled with a tiny spark of envy. Emma sank her chin
into her hands. 'I think I'll make a scrummy chocolate mousse.'

'Mm. It's my very favourite.'

'I know. The twins' too. I wonder who they take
after?'

Changed into jeans and a cool cotton shirt, it was
good to walk briskly along the narrow country lanes
into the nearby village. Pippa had purposely left
her hair loose and a warm breeze stirred it gently
against her neck. Whether it was the sun or the
change of surroundings she didn't know, but it was
good to feel herself beginning to relax and unwind.
With all its complications, St Clement's might have
been another world, and that was how she preferred it. There was safety in distance. Not, she
reflected crossly with herself, that she was at all
sure precisely what it was she was escaping from.

She tucked her hands into her pockets and stared
at the sea but, annoyingly, it was Julius Sterling's

face which seemed to lap, unasked and certainly uninvited, into her thoughts, taking the pleasurable edge off the afternoon.

She quickened her step purposefully. A weekend wasn't long enough to put her ruffled emotions in order, but it was all she had.

Shopping completed, she ignored the twice-weekly bus and walked back. The sun had lost some of its warmth and the tide had come in, covering the fine golden sand. The exercise had done her good, blowing away the cobwebs, and Pippa felt her appetite stir at the thought of food. It would be nice to be able to relax and chat to Emma and Garrard, and she felt a tiny surge of pleasure as she turned into the drive to see the large black car already parked in front of the house. So he had managed to get home early after all.

Flushed after the exercise, she went through to the kitchen, depositing the fish and the rest of the shopping, pausing in the hall just long enough to glance in the mirror before going to the sitting-room from where she could hear voices. Her cheeks were warm and the sun had emphasised her freckles and taken away some of the pallor she seemed to have acquired over the past few weeks. She toyed briefly with the idea of rushing upstairs to change out of the old jeans, worn into comfortable shabbiness, and decided it could wait until she had said a proper hello.

Dragging a hand through her windswept hair, she walked into the room, a smile on her lips, to see Emma pouring tea. The twins were both ensconced in bouncing chairs which were living up to their names and Garrard stood talking to someone else. A figure who frowned as his attention was diverted from the conversation by her own slightly breath-less entrance.

For what seemed an endless moment her heart did a crazy sort of double-take as the smile slid from her lips.

'Ah, here she is at last.' Garrard was drawing her relentlessly forward. 'Pippa, we've got another visi-tor for the weekend. An old friend of mine from way back in medical school. It was quite amazing. We met again today, quite by chance. Julius, come and meet my little sister-in-law, Pippa.'

She felt her hand being clasped, was aware of the cool gaze which seemed to regard her steadily with some expression which she couldn't—wasn't even sure she wanted to—read. 'Nurse Benedict, I presume.'

Her mouth opened. 'S . . . sir.' Her brain ham-mered the thought that it wasn't fair. He had no right to be here, to intrude.

'Don't tell me you two know each other?'

She dragged her hand away and heard him say quietly, 'Our paths have crossed from time to time. It must be fate, don't you think, Nurse?'

Was he laughing at her? If so, there was no sign of it in the cool gaze which seemed to take in her slim figure in the tight jeans which suddenly felt too shabby and awful for words.

'I . . . I suppose it must be.' She tore her glance from his face to notice Emma studying her with amused curiosity.

'Oh well, in that case you don't have to be horribly formal. I couldn't bear to listen to the pair of you calling each other "Nurse" and "Sir" all weekend. It would be too silly for words. Pippa, this is Julius. Julius, this is Pippa. Now, shall we all

have some fresh tea? Come on, Pippa. We may as
well leave these men to talk shop for five minutes.'

It was a relief to find herself whisked away to the
kitchen where she drew deep breaths and tried to
recover something of her shattered composure.
How was she going to face the rest of the weekend?
It was bad enough on the wards, where at least
formality created barriers of its own, but here . . .
She looked desperately at Emma.

'I've been thinking; perhaps I ought to get back
first thing in the morning. I've got so much to get
ready before I go on to the ward on Monday.'

'Nonsense.' Emma was busy loading cakes on to
a plate. 'You've only just got here. We haven't
even had a chance to have a real gossip and I'm
dying to catch up on all the news. Besides,' she
flicked a glance at Pippa's white face, 'what do you
imagine Julius would think if you upped and left
now?'

He'd probably be highly delighted, Pippa
thought miserably. He was probably every bit as
anxious to put the memory of that last encounter
behind him as she was, even if it was for different
reasons. The fact that he had kissed her on the spur
of the moment was something he would probably
far rather forget. Well, he needn't worry on that
score. She had no intention of letting him think she
had given it even a second's further thought. If only
it were true, some demon persisted. 'Did you know
him?' She picked up a tea towel and polished a cup
so hard that Emma removed it from her grasp.

'Aren't you overdoing that just a little?' She put
the cup on the tray. 'No, as a matter of fact I didn't.
I've never seen him before, but he's rather dishy,
isn't he? Actually Garrard rang to say he'd met an

old friend who was attending the conference down here and was bringing him home. He did mention that he worked at Clem's so I was delighted, naturally, but it didn't occur to me . . .' She broke off, suddenly conscious of the flushed face in front of her. 'Pippa . . . he's not the one? You don't mean . . ?'

Pippa busied herself at the sink. 'Yes he is, and it's horribly embarrassing.'

'But I thought from the way you spoke that he was some kind of monster. Are you sure we're talking about the same man? He looks quite harmless.'

'Well that just goes to prove how looks can deceive.' She sniffed miserably. Harmless was not an adjective she would apply to Julius Sterling under any circumstances. She dried her hands briskly. 'Honestly, of all the luck. Trust me to pick this weekend of all weekends. I shouldn't have come. It's going to be unbearable.'

'But we couldn't possibly have known, and anyway it's only for a couple of days so it's not so bad. It's not as if you're at work, so what can possibly happen in that time?'

It was a question Pippa preferred not even to think about as she splashed cold water on her face. 'Look, I'll go and change first, if you don't mind.'

'Of course not, but you look fine.'

'Thanks, but I feel a bit windswept. It won't take a minute to step into something else.' Though she wasn't at all sure why she bothered, as she slipped out of the jeans and into a cool, mint green cotton dress which seemed to do things for the colour of her eyes. It certainly wasn't for Julius Sterling's benefit. He probably didn't recognise anyone who didn't wear a uniform anyway. A thought which didn't quite bring the relief she had hoped for, somehow, as she made her way slowly downstairs.

The rest of the afternoon and evening was something of a nightmare. The twins screamed. The fish was delicious but the chocolate mousse had refused to set and Emma finally rushed upstairs looking distinctly watery-eyed, clutching a baby in each arm, closely followed by Garrard looking pale and grimly thoughtful.

Pippa sat at the table, suddenly all too conscious of the man opposite. It was amazing how different he looked in casual slacks and sweater, an image which took her by surprise and left her feeling oddly uncomfortable. Beyond the diffused light of the candles she caught the outline of his profile and he seemed younger, more relaxed. She had even heard him laugh, and she had found herself watching, fascinated by the metamorphosis which had brought with it a sharp pang of realisation that he was very attractive.

It came as a shock to realise that he was speaking and she hadn't been taking in a single word. It was ridiculous to find her heart thudding and she had been grateful when the conversation had drifted on around her, no one noticing that she was quiet or didn't eat much.

She jumped as he spoke, smiling at her from behind the glow of the candles. 'It seems we've been left to our own devices. I'm sure it's only a minor family crisis. Shall we take our coffee into the other room? Your sister said something about drinks. Perhaps you'd like a brandy?'

'No thanks.' Pippa leapt to her feet as he moved round the table, aware of the unevenness of her voice. 'Not for me, thanks, but you go ahead. I think I'll just clear some of these dishes.'

She began feverishly to gather up plates until his hand closed over hers. 'Leave them.' It was a command and he was frowning. 'Let's talk instead.'

She swallowed hard, refusing to look at him, to be moved by his nearness and the effect it was having. 'I was under the impression that that was what we'd been doing all evening.'

'On the contrary. I thought that was precisely what you had been avoiding—that you would rather be anywhere than here, having to make conversation with me.' His gaze was fixed on her face and there was an expression in his eyes she couldn't even begin to interpret. 'What exactly are you afraid of?'

Even to her own ears her laugh sounded false, uneasy. 'I really don't know what you mean. Why on earth should I be afraid?'

'I've no idea. You tell me, Pippa.'

She flinched as his hand touched her arm, sending a tingling sensation running through it. 'You're imagining things.'

'Am I? Look at me.' He tilted her chin up so that she had no choice but to obey, and wished she hadn't as her heartbeat quickened. 'Am I really so difficult to like?'

She couldn't look at him.

'Well, am I?'

She bit her lip, snatching her hand away from his grasp as she bent to blow out the candles. Anything rather than have him see the tears which welled up suddenly. 'No, of course not.'

'Then what is it?' He stopped her before she could reach the other candle and a shiver went through her as his hand came down on her arm.

'I . . . it's nothing. I'm just tired, I expect. We've been working pretty hard in PTS these past few weeks, despite what you may think.' She said it purposely with a hint of flippancy, challenging him to laugh, but his face was quite serious, even angry, as he looked at her.

'We're not at the hospital now, Pippa, and I hope we're not going to go through the ridiculous farce of you calling me sir and practically standing to attention every time I look at you for the rest of the weekend.'

She swallowed hard. 'Habit dies hard.'

'Bad habits should be broken.'

But it wasn't that simple, she thought, forcing a laugh. 'You've forgotten what it's like to be one of the downtrodden.'

'On the contrary.' His mouth was a grim line. 'I remember very well, but I fail to see what it has to do with the situation here and now. When I leave the hospital I leave my work behind. I do have a private existence, you know.'

She closed her eyes, not wanting to know. It was far, far safer to think of him as an anonymous figure.

'Contrary to what you may think, even doctors have feelings. A white coat doesn't offer some sort of magical immunity, much as there are times when I might wish it did.'

His voice was very soft, his face so close. She could smell the tantalising aroma of aftershave. She drew in a shaking breath, her lips parted, drawn, as if by some stronger power, towards his mouth, willing the kiss yet afraid of what it would stir up. What did he mean, 'much as he might wish it'? Her eyes flew open. What was she thinking of? Shock propelled her from the danger area. He might be off duty but he was still the senior consultant and she was still a nurse, a student at that, and on Monday she would have to work with him again.

She blushed furiously at the thought of how nearly she had made a fool of herself.

'Pippa, what's wrong?'

She couldn't bear to look at him. 'Nothing. Nothing at all. I've got a headache, that's all.'

She heard him call out as she fled, but didn't stop. She was learning quickly that cowardice was her strongest suit where he was concerned, and it wasn't a quality she liked in herself at all.

In the safety of her bedroom she sat with her face in her hands, breathing hard. The weekend suddenly seemed to stretch endlessly ahead and she wasn't at all sure how she was going to endure the remainder.

CHAPTER EIGHT

PIPPA SLEPT badly and woke early. She lay quietly for a long time, until she decided to dress and slip out of the house to go for a brisk walk in the hope that it would help to get rid of a headache. There was something utterly beautiful about the crisp chill of the morning before the sun finally came up, and she felt herself gradually beginning to relax as she plodded in silence down the narrow road towards the little cove. Her shoes crunched over a ridge of shingle as she walked towards the sea, bending to skim a pebble across the waves, watching it sink without trace. The thought hovered, uncomfortably, that it would be much the same if she were to leave Clem's and walk out of the consultant's life. He wouldn't even notice she'd gone. It would all go on as if she'd never been there.

She pushed the hair from her eyes, shivering, and wished she had brought a jacket instead of just the thick, bright red sweater. The trouble was, she sighed as she turned to walk along the beach, she wasn't at all sure she had the courage to walk out.

Lying awake, tossing and turning last night, only one thing had emerged from a tormenting jumble of thoughts—and that was that she was in love with Julius Sterling. Pippa didn't know how it had happened, but the realisation had sent her sitting bolt upright in bed until finally she had dozed, only to dream that she was being kissed. She had woken to feel her cheeks burning and a painful realisation that it hadn't been real. After that she had given up all thought of sleep. Sleep meant dreams, and she preferred to have full control of any situation which involved the senior consultant. He wasn't going to be given the chance to creep up on her again.

'Good morning. You're out early. What's the matter, couldn't sleep?'

The pebble flew from her hand as if jet-propelled as she whirled round to meet the mocking gaze. Julius was dressed in slacks and black sweater and seemed totally oblivious to the cold which, she suddenly knew, had maliciously made her own nose and cheeks glow. She bent quickly for another stone, aiming it with calculated deliberation at the water before deigning to answer. It sank with a dull plop and she was furious to see the suspicion of laughter in his eyes.

'Actually, I'm always up early,' she lied brightly, through clenched teeth. 'It's the best part of the day, don't you think?'

'I do.' He shamed her by skimming a stone effortlessly across the waves in what she considered was an unnecessary display of male chauvinism. 'But then I find it's the only time in the day when I get peace and quiet and time to think. It's important.'

Pippa studied him surreptitiously, seeing the faint lines etched at his eyes and mouth and wondered what he thought about, what it was that made such a man feel the need to be alone. Suddenly she felt she was the intruder, and the thought rankled because she had been the one looking for escape and he had been the one to destroy it.

'Well, I won't disturb you then. I came out for a walk. I need the exercise.'

'Do you? I wouldn't have thought so.' His gaze raked her body in the figure-hugging jeans. 'Obviously you don't go in for the hospital stodge.'

'Don't you believe it,' she retaliated defensively. 'I'm always at the head of the queue.'

'Really? It doesn't show.'

Pippa sensed that he was deliberately teasing and was glad of the wind whipping the colour into her cheeks. 'As a matter of fact, I'm stoking up an appetite for breakfast. I promised myself a brisk trot from one end of the cove to the other.' She stood jogging on the spot, hoping he would believe it was enthusiasm rather than cold which made her too scared to stand still in case she froze.

He stared past her to the distant outcrop of rocks. 'I'd forget it if I were you. You'll never make it.'

Her mouth opened indignantly. Suddenly the one thing she was determined to do more than anything was to show him that she didn't give a damn for his male chauvinist advice. 'I'm not exactly helpless, you know. I won the five hundred metres at school, and the relay.'

His mouth twitched. 'That must have been ages ago. I'd still forget it if I were you.'

'Nonsense. I can make it in ten minutes.'

'Somehow I doubt that.' He nodded behind her. 'Unless, of course, you also happened to win the school breast-stroke.'

Pippa turned and gasped. The tide, which had looked so innocent, had encroached insidiously up over the sands without her being aware of it, and she felt herself shudder at the thought that she might so easily have been cut off. 'You knew,' she accused hotly, as if it were his fault.

'Not exactly,' he said with infuriating calm. 'I watched you from the cliff tops. I guessed you didn't realise what was happening.'

'Well then, why didn't you warn me?'

'My dear girl, I've been trying to attract your attention from the cliff top for the past ten minutes—but you were obviously far too engrossed in a world of your own.'

Pippa's hands clenched with humiliation in her pockets. 'Well, I could still make it easily. The tide won't be in fully for ages yet, in fact it probably doesn't come all the way up.'

'Don't be a little idiot, you'd be asking for trouble.'

'How dare you?' She flung a look of fury in his direction and almost succumbed to the gleam in his own eyes, except that she wouldn't let him think he had won. Her eyes scanned the narrowing line of sand. She could still make it, just about . . . with a lot of luck. 'I really don't need you to tell me what to do. We're not at the hospital now, you know. I'm perfectly free to do as I please, and I don't need your permission.'

There was something ominous in the way he moved to stand barring her path. The grim line of his mouth seemed to belie the coolness of his voice as he said, 'I don't want to dispute the issue, but I have no intention of letting you make a fool of yourself and even less, I assure you, of being obliged to come to your rescue when you find yourself in danger of drowning.'

Her heart thudded. She wasn't sure whether it was fury or his nearness that was having the effect of making her feel light-headed. Perhaps she should have had breakfast before she came out.

She faced him, chin up, eyes blazing.

'And I assure you I'm perfectly capable of taking care of myself, Mr Sterling.' She turned her back on him, preparing to head along the beach. It was a mistake. In what seemed to be a single fluid movement which took her breath away, she felt herself lifted bodily into the air and suffered the humiliation of finding herself thrust over his shoulder as he turned to stride angrily back along the beach and began the long haul up the cliff path. She knew he was angry by the sound of his breathing, but the sheer indignity of finding herself treated like a sack of potatoes was too much to bear. Just who did he think he was? Her fists thudded into his back.

'Put me down you . . . you beast!' Tears of mortification and rage stung at her eyes, leaving him utterly impervious. Her hand reached for and found the soft darkness of his hair, and she tugged with the sheer elation of revenge, which was short-lived—for with a soft oath he reached up, imprisoning her wrist in a vice-like grip, and jerked her with a breath-stopping thud even further over his shoulder.

'Don't try that again, young woman, or I'll give you the spanking of your life.'

'You wouldn't dare!' The words were jerked from her. Then she was suddenly dropped to her feet as they reached the cliff top and she stood fighting for breath, trying desperately to regain some shred of dignity as she faced him. 'I hate you. You had no right . . .'

'My dear girl, don't ever dare me. Next time I might just let you go ahead and drown yourself.'

She swallowed convulsively. 'Don't be ridiculous. You're exaggerating. I wasn't in any danger, except from you.'

His mouth twisted, dangerously lazy. 'Ah, I wondered if you'd realised that.'

Pippa wondered if she had imagined it, that slight twitching at the corners of his mouth; then he jerked his head roughly in the direction of the beach where she had walked only a quarter of an hour before. Suddenly she felt cold. The sand was gone. She looked at him. 'How could you possibly know?'

'Quite simply—the water line can be seen clearly on the rocks. And as it happens, Garrard mentioned to me, in passing, that the tide can be quite treacherous in some of these coves. That's probably why the tourists avoid them.'

Pippa stood in miserable silence and suddenly his hands reached down to clasp her frozen fingers, drawing her closer. She sniffed hard. 'I hate you.'

A slight frown cut its way into his craggy features and the wind blew his hair until she felt a desperate urge to brush it from his eyes.

'Do you, Pippa?' he said softly. 'Why is that, I wonder?'

'Because . . .' She wished he would let her go. 'You're doing it again, confusing me.'

'I can't imagine why.' His face was very close, tanned, arrogant . . . dangerous.

Whether by accident or design, his hand moved to brush against her cheek and she shivered involuntarily.

'You're cold. Come on, we'd better get you back to the house before you end up with hypothermia, and then I'd probably blame myself for that too.'

She didn't give a thought to what he meant as he

bundled her along the road towards the house, his arm round her to stop her shivering, except that somehow it only seemed to make things worse.

They burst in through the door, windswept and breathless, to find Emma looking very pale and sleepy as she fed the twins their breakfast. She looked up and smiled. 'My goodness, some people have lots of energy. I didn't hear the pair of you go out. Enjoy your stroll?'

'Mm, it was lovely,' Pippa murmured brightly, casting a furious look in Julius's direction.

His eyes gleamed briefly. 'I'd like to make a habit of it, if only I had the time and opportunity.'

'Well, you must come down more often. We'd be pleased to see you any time.'

Pippa ground her teeth together. 'I'm sure Mr Sterling has far too much to do.'

'Oh, I expect I can always make a little time, if I try very hard,' he murmured with annoying deliberation close to her ear. She flung him a look of hatred which somehow didn't quite come out right, and stormed up to her room to comb her hair and change her sweater.

When she emerged ten minutes later, it was to find him sitting calmly in the kitchen eating bacon and eggs, for all the world as if it was the habit of a lifetime. *His wife must look after him jolly well*. The thought came from nowhere and suddenly Pippa found herself staring at him, feeling as if someone had stabbed her with a knife. His wife. Why hadn't it occurred to her before, the possibility that he might be married? Of course he would be, a man like that. It was funny she hadn't heard anything on the grapevine—but then, she sensed that Julius Sterling was a man who liked to keep his private life just that, and that very few people ever got close to the real man unless he chose to let them.

'Are you all right?' A brief look of concern flitted over his features and she blushed, annoyed that he had caught her staring.

'What? Oh . . . yes, thanks.'

'You should have had more sense than to go out without a jacket.'

'Well, I'll certainly remember in future,' she hissed, refusing the offer of bacon and helping herself to bread to make toast.

The twins were in good voice. David stoically munched his way through a dish of cereal while Katy plastered hers into her curls and seemed to think the whole thing was great fun. 'I think she has the idea it's meant to be administered from the outside,' Emma wailed, grabbing a cloth and wiping the spotty face.

'Well, they certainly look brighter this morning.'

Pippa wondered if it was a personal or professional opinion as Julius said it. Somehow she gained the impression he missed nothing, which was a pity because her own face glowed like a lantern after the morning's exercise. She was giving the toast her undivided attention when Garrard walked into the kitchen, dressed in his formal dark suit and carrying a briefcase.

'Oh, you're not working?'

''Fraid so. I've a couple of patients I must see. It shouldn't take long though. Sorry about this.' He glanced ruefully in Julius's direction.

'Not to worry. I know what it's like only too well. Would you like me to come along?'

'Would you care to?'

'Very much, if I won't be in the way.'

Garrard laughed. 'Far from it. As a matter of fact, I've a case I'd value your opinion on.' He looked at his watch. 'Can you be ready in half an hour?'

'Easily.'

Garrard turned to his wife and the twins. 'Hello, poppets.' He embraced all three until Emma blushed and rushed from the room, muttering something about clean nappies and powder. Watching her, Pippa felt yet another pang of envy. It was all so perfect and so impossible.

Garrard poured himself a cup of coffee and stood to drink it. He looked vaguely uneasy. She offered him a piece of toast.

'You're not worried about the twins, are you?'

'Oh good lord, no. The worst's over, I should think. It's been a bit hard on Emma though. Two babies can be a handful at the best of times, but when they're not well . . .' He looked at them both. 'As a matter of fact, I was thinking that what she really needs is a break. Just a couple of hours to get away from babies and nappies.'

'I agree wholeheartedly.' Julius surveyed his friend calmly. 'So why don't you take her out for a while this evening, while we're here to do the honours?'

Garrard grinned sheepishly. 'Are you sure you wouldn't mind? I was going to ask, but didn't quite know how to go about it.'

'For heaven's sake, man, take your wife out! You both deserve it. I should think we can cope with a couple of infants, don't you, Pippa?'

Julius was watching her as a predator watches its prey, and she felt the colour wash up into her face at the thought of being trapped, alone with him, for an entire evening.

'Y . . . yes, of course we can,' she heard herself say. 'I think it's a marvellous idea.' An even better one hovered traitorously in the back of her mind. She could pack her case and catch the first train back to Clem's. 'Make the most of it. We'll be fine. Just leave bottles and nappies at the ready and go. I'm sure we can handle a couple of babies.'

Whether she could handle the rest of the evening was quite another matter. She stared miserably at her toast and reached for the marmalade to take the sudden dryness out of her throat.

'We'll have to do this more often.'

She choked on her coffee as the softy spoken words reached her across the table, but Julius was studying the morning paper, an enigmatic expression on his face which told her absolutely nothing.

'I've made up bottles, just in case. They tend to wake up feeling a bit hot and thirsty while they aren't well. Nappies are in the cupboard there. Oh, and David likes his teddy if he wakes up.' Emma leaned over the cots to stare at the sleeping babies and frowned. 'Katy feels a bit hot, don't you think? Her cheek looks quite flushed. Perhaps I ought to stay . . .'

Pippa touched the child lightly with her own hand. 'She's warm, not hot, and her teeth are probably bothering her. Honestly, Emma, you're getting yourself into a state for nothing. I'm here, and if there's any kind of emergency I have the telephone number of the restaurant and I promise I'll ring you. Why don't you just go out, enjoy yourselves? Garrard could do with a break too.'

'Oh yes, I know. He's marvellous, but . . .'
Emma still hesitated. 'I suppose you're right. I
know I'm being silly, but I've never left them
before.' She sighed, switching off the light. 'Still,
you've got Julius here as well. He jolly well ought to
know what to do.'

Yes, Pippa thought as they made their way
downstairs, she had Julius, and the prospect was
daunting to say the least.

'He's rather nice, isn't he?' Emma hunted in her
bag for a lipstick.

'Who?'

'Julius, silly.'

'Oh, I suppose so. I hadn't really noticed. He's
not my type.'

Emma looked at her flushed cheeks and hid a
smile. 'I thought the two of you were getting along
very well when you came in this morning looking all
bright-eyed and bushy-tailed. Of course, Garrard's
known him for ages. He says even in medical school
he was always tipped to do well, and he's brilliant at
hearts.'

'I'm sure he is, Pippa thought, feeling suddenly
quite desolate. But he's not doing a great job for
mine right now.

In the sitting-room Garrard was hovering ner-
vously. 'You're sure you don't mind?'

Julius stirred from his seat in front of the fire
where he looked ridiculously at home. 'I hope
you're not casting aspersions at my ability to cope
with two mere nine-month-old infants? I think it
would take a lot more than that to defeat me,
especially with the efficient Nurse Benedict to offer
such able assistance.'

Pippa threw him a glowering look and turned her

back on him as she ushered Emma and Garrard out of the door. 'They're both fine. I know where everything is. The telephone number is right next to the phone, and if you don't go now you're going to lose your table.'

They went, not without a last, anxious wave from Emma, and Pippa returned to the sitting-room to find the lights lowered and Julius sprawled on the sofa, staring at the television. He looked harmless enough, she thought, and sat in a chair as far away as possible with a book, which she grabbed from the shelf in a desperate attempt to appear occupied, and made a determined effort to read.

It wasn't the television which was disturbing. It was far more that his presence engendered a kind of intimacy to the scene which was too disquieting for comfort. He looked so utterly relaxed, she thought, peering at him over the book. Hands clasped on his stomach, long legs casually relaxed, laughter playing at the corners of his mouth as he watched some outrageous soap opera, he bore no resemblance to the man she had encountered earlier. She was glad of the subdued lighting as her cheeks coloured. He needn't think she was fooled for one minute. Julius Sterling was a dangerous animal. She couldn't say much for the state of her own emotions either!

It was several seconds before she realised that his attention had left the screen and that he was watching her with lazy amusement. 'You'd be far more comfortable here, you know. There's plenty of room.' He patted the sofa beside him and she deliberately plumped the cushion behind her with nervous enthusiasm.

'This is fine, thanks.'

He studied her through half-closed eyes. 'Is that

why you've been fidgeting like an angry kitten for the past half-hour?'

'I haven't,' she protested. 'I've been reading. It's a jolly good book if you must know.'

A nerve pulsed in his jaw. 'I'm sure it must be. You've read all of one page.' He leaned forward and without warning snatched the book from her hands. His mouth twisted. 'Mm, a manual of operating techniques. All stirring stuff, but just a little out of your line, wouldn't you say?'

She launched herself to her feet. 'Not at all,' she snapped frostily. 'We all have to start somewhere.'

Again she sensed the quiet laughter as he rose to his feet too. 'Ah, you must forgive me. I hadn't realised you were planning to go into surgery. Not that I don't commend it, I just think perhaps you're being a little ambitious at this stage.'

She snatched the book back, glaring furiously. 'Well if you must know, I can't stand the hospital hearts and flowers stuff.'

This time he laughed outright and bent to click the switch on the TV. 'Well, I'm glad to hear that. I was beginning to think I'd have to endure a whole evening of it.'

Her mouth fell open. 'But you were watching it!'

'My dear girl, only because I thought it was what you would want. I imagined females like that kind of thing.'

'Well I don't.' Her voice shook. 'I think it's ridiculous the way they behave as if those doctors were gods. They can't operate without a full orchestra crashing in the background and if I see another nurse flashing inch-long eye-lashes and looking like something out of *Vogue* I shall . . . I shall be sick.'

'My, my, you feel quite strongly about it, don't you?'

'Yes. Yes I do.'

His brows rose fractionally. 'Well, it's nice to see that at least someone has the medical profession in proper perspective. I've never understood the glamorous image of it myself. I don't see doctors as the strong silent hero type, but then, that's probably because we really know what goes on. We see the pain and the failures, don't we, not just the acceptable, clean side of it.'

'Yes, I suppose we do,' Pippa murmured lamely, thinking with considerable annoyance that in his case, the strong silent image had never been more appropriate.

'Would you like a drink?'

'I thought I'd make some coffee.' She fled with the excuse to the kitchen, taking as long as was humanly possible to make two cups, returning to have him look at her quizzically as she set the tray in front of him on the coffee table.

'You don't have to keep avoiding me, you know. I don't bite.' He ignored the sugar and she ladled three large spoonfuls into her own, wincing as she took a sip.

'I didn't imagine you did.' She almost added that it wasn't his bite she was afraid of, but stared at the clock instead. Perhaps Emma would fret about the twins and come home early. Perhaps she could go and wake them up and phone the restaurant. 'They won't be home for hours.'

'No, I don't imagine they will. I hope they make the most of it.'

Pippa blinked foolishly, not even aware that she had spoken the words aloud, carried the cups back to the kitchen and took even longer to wash them up. Perhaps he would fall asleep. She heard music drifting through softly, something classical which she vaguely recognised. He had obviously put a record on. It was sweetly, savagely, romantic and she closed her eyes, despising the weakness of her own emotions which suddenly made her long to be in his arms.

'I've been up to check the babies.'

Pippa spun round to find Julius standing behind her. She stubbornly refused to let her eyes meet his and stared instead at his hair, curling gently against the neck of his sweater. The kitchen sink was digging painfully into her back, but she couldn't move because he was far too close.

'P-perhaps I should change their nappies, or . . . something.'

He shook his head. 'I don't think that would be a good idea right now, do you?'

'N . . . no.' His eyes were incredibly blue.

'I have a much better one.' His head moved closer. 'My darling girl, what am I going to do about you?'

Her hands dug into the metal behind her as his lips came down gently over her own. She stood frozen, willing herself not to react as his mouth searched and teased, dragging responses from her until she drew in a long, shuddering breath and her arms reached up to his neck. She could feel the warmth of his body through the thin sweater, the lithe muscular physique, which suddenly became much more demanding as he drew her relentlessly closer and closer still, until her lips parted in a reckless invitation. He moaned softly, his hands digging painfully into her flesh.

A distant wail dragged her, lethargically, back to reality. The music, she thought. Must be the end of the record. The wail was joined by another. She jerked back, still held in his embrace, feeling the combined thud of two hearts. 'Oh no, the twins! I'd better go.'

He was up the stairs ahead of her and they stood side by side in the doorway of the nursery, breaking into quiet laughter at the sight of two flushed little faces standing smiling through the bars of their cots.

'Saved by the babies, I think.' She heard the barely audible retort and tore her gaze away as they each headed for an infant.

She couldn't help but agree and yet, perversely, she felt miserable. 'So near and yet so far,' she whispered to the down-soft cheek against hers. 'Oh well, I expect he's relieved. He certainly moved fast enough to get away.'

Later that night, lying in bed, Pippa went over the evening in searching detail which became gradually more and more befuddled until she turned over and pulled the sheet over her head. So what happened? she asked herself. 'Nothing happened, except that he kissed me and there's no point in reading anything into that.' A man like Julius Sterling must have kissed dozens of women. She decided it was a thought better not pursued, much as she might have liked to. In any case, he had made it quite clear that he kept his business and private lives totally separate, and on Monday she would go back to being Student Nurse Benedict and he would be the senior consultant.

She went down to breakfast next morning feeling heavy-eyed and nurturing the beginnings of a headache, to find Emma feeding the twins. 'Hi! You certainly look better for your night out.'

'Mm, it was marvellous. I actually felt quite guilty.'

'Idiot. You should do it more often. It must be possible to find a good reliable baby-sitter every once in a while.'

'I know. That's what Garrard said. It's just that I've more or less resisted the idea, until now. Still, since you managed so beautifully I might be persuaded.'

'I should think so too. Anyway, they weren't any trouble at all. All they wanted were clean nappies and a drink of juice and Julius dealt with one while I did the other. I must say he certainly seemed efficient.' Pippa glanced at the clock. 'Where is he, by the way? Don't tell me, out at the crack of dawn to jog along the beach!'

'Actually,' Emma stirred two dishes of baby cereal, 'he isn't. Of course, you don't know—there was an early call from the hospital.'

'Clem's, you mean?'

'Mm, an emergency of some kind. He didn't say what. I heard him talking to Garrard then he came in, looking very tense. He muttered something about a personal matter he had to attend to and asked if I'd make his apologies to you for having to rush back and leave you to make your own way home. He didn't see why you should have to lose the last day of your weekend with us. And very nice of him too, if I may say so—from my point of view, anyway. It's been lovely having you here. Do try and come again soon. I've hardly had a chance to gossip at all.'

'I'll try.' Pippa stirred her coffee, trying very

hard not to feel cheated. She had steeled herself to seeing him, to facing the look in those expressive eyes, wondering whether she had misread what had been there last night. And now he was gone. 'I don't know when my first official weekend off will be. You know how it is. Sister makes up the duty rota and if my luck's out it could be a month.'

'Well, let me know. I can't think where the weekend's gone. It's so unfair.'

It was indeed, Pippa thought as she stared out of the train window at passing fields and the steadily encroaching town. It had disappeared with all the hazy unreality of a dream, except that one tangible thing remained, the fact that she loved Julius Sterling.

She sighed heavily and leaned back, closing her eyes. It was probably as well she had had to make her own way back. Her emotions had taken a considerable battering and his presence was scarcely conducive to bringing them back under control.

CHAPTER NINE

'WE HAVE nine patients for Theatre today.' Sister Travers's gaze moved steadily from one uniformed figure to the other as they crowded into the small office. 'It means we're all going to have to stay on our toes and will not be used as an excuse for laxness. Urgent dressings will be attended to as usual. The more routine ones may have to wait a little, but no patient, I repeat, *no* patient is to be subjected to any discomfort simply because a nurse doesn't have time. You will make time—is that clearly understood?'

There were varying nods and murmurs of assent before they filed back on to the ward to begin the ritual of taking over, and from the moment the last of the night staff left, nurses were scurrying in all directions until Pippa felt as if her head was spinning. All the beds had to be stripped and re-made. There were several blanket baths to be given, medicines to be handed out and two patients sent up to Theatre, all before the mid-morning drinks were served.

Pippa found herself going for her own coffee in a kind of daze and Liz met her with two cups and a look of sympathy as they headed through the crowd towards an empty table.

'Hi, how did the weekend go? Judging from the looks of you, I can't say you seem to have benefited greatly.'

Pippa stifled a yawn, drank the scalding liquid

and winced. 'Actually it was very nice. The babies are gorgeous. A touch spotty. A sudden plague of measles descended just in time to coincide with my arrival.'

'Oh lor! Look well if you get it. You do look a bit peaky.'

'I've had it.' Pippa added more sugar to her cup with concentrated deliberation. 'It's probably a cold coming. I'm sure I had measles when I was small. I must have. I had everything else that was going. Anyway, I should be so lucky! A couple of weeks off now would suit me very nicely.'

'I know the feeling.' Liz leaned back, stretching her legs, easing aching calf-muscles. 'From what I've seen of Women's Med so far, it's going to be a hard stint and Sister's a real tartar.'

'I thought we had the worst of it on Men's Surgical. Travers lacks only the jackboots. The whip may be metaphorical, but she cracks it with the efficiency of a medieval torturer. I'll be glad when Carson gets back from leave, but I shall probably be a nervous wreck long before then,' Pippa said gloomily.

'I'm seriously beginning to think they're all made from the same mould. You know, little Sister clones, dropping off the end of a production line somewhere. They just give them different names and march them off to the wards to make our lives a misery. Pretty much like doctors, really. How's that lovely brother-in-law of yours, by the way?'

Pippa took a large bite out of a biscuit. 'Still gorgeous. Thoroughly besotted, of course, but then I can't blame him. Emma is absolutely thriving on marriage and motherhood.'

'Well who wouldn't? Chance would be a nice thing though.' Liz yawned and grimaced. 'I suppose I'd better get back. Perhaps I'll see you at lunch.'

'Heaven knows! I shouldn't think it's likely. We're up to our eyes. Nine for ops and Sister's keeping a beady eye on all of us, so I don't know when I'll get off.'

They parted on the stairs and Pippa carried on to the next floor, arriving on the ward to find Sister Travers waiting for her, her gaze rising pointedly to the wall clock. Rebellion stirred briefly in Pippa's breast. She can look all she likes, she thought. I'm on time and she jolly well knows it. In fact I'm a minute early.

'Nurse, I want you to go down to X-ray straight away and ask what's happened to Mr Roberts's plates. Mr Sterling particularly asked for them for this morning's round, so go and stir them up please—and be quick about it.'

'Yes, Sister.' She fled, trying desperately to convince herself as she ran down the stairs again that the sudden quickening of her heartbeat was due entirely to the exercise. So he was back. The personal business, whatever it was, must have resolved itself. Pippa experienced a sudden and quite ridiculous surge of joy, which vanished as quickly as it had come. What possible difference did she think it could make? As far as he was concerned, the weekend had probably already faded into insignificance. He would have assumed his place behind the barrier and she must do the same, if that were humanly possible.

She strode into X-ray, which was in its usual chaotic state with patients in wheelchairs bumping

into those who could walk, and various members of
staff trying to deal with each in turn.

'I could have sworn we sent those plates up.' A
harassed clerk ran through the file again. 'I'm sure
we did.'

'Well Sister hasn't had them, and they are
needed for this morning's round.'

'You did say Mrs D Roberts?'

'No, actually it's *Mr*. Men's Surgical. At least,
I hope for his sake he is, otherwise we're in
trouble.'

The clerk scratched his head. 'Oh damn! In that
case these are yours. Heaven knows why someone
doesn't come up with a better system. It would
make life a lot easier all round.'

Pippa left him to it. The intricacies of hospital
administration were definitely not her department.

'Mr Roberts's X-rays, Sister.'

'Thank goodness for that. Why don't they get
themselves sorted out down there? Put them with
the other case notes in the trolley, Nurse, and tidy
those bed-curtains round Mr Warren's bed. And
those papers.' She tutted crossly. 'This ward is a
mess.'

Pippa straightened the curtains, rearranged pillows and removed discarded newspapers from
locker-tops. 'Sorry, Mr Warren. We have to look
tidy for the doctors' rounds,' she smiled in answer
to a complaint as she tucked the offending items out
of sight. 'Sister's orders, I'm afraid.'

He climbed back into bed, shedding his dressing-
gown. 'Can't see what all the fuss is about. He
comes to look at the patients, doesn't he?'

She had to agree, though silently of course. 'Just
bear with it, Mr Warren. With a bit of luck you'll be

going out in a few days, then you won't have to worry about our silly rules and regulations.'

She straightened up, catching Sister's eye, and blushed as the swing doors opened, bringing a flock of attentive, white-faced medical students in the wake of the very figure she had determinedly been telling herself she would not look for. All the same, her heart gave a discomforting lurch of pleasure as she bent her flushed cheeks quickly to the unnecessary task of tucking in bedclothes.

'Mr Sterling, we're quite ready for you, sir.' Caroline Travers bustled towards him, case notes efficiently at the ready, the first deposited neatly into his hand before he could ask for them.

For a second Pippa felt an unreasoned pang of envy for even that slight contact seniority brought. Then she straightened up as he moved down the ward in her direction, a smile hovering on her lips.

He was studying the notes as he paused at the bed, a frown of concentration biting into the good-looking features. Standing quietly with her hands behind her back, she was conscious of a sudden, overwhelming sense of shyness as she studied the strong profile, the face which could appear so autocratic and yet which could also relax into lines of teasing laughter. Was it really possible that only hours ago he had looked down at her, kissed her in a way that had left her feeling breathless and quite convinced that beneath the formal dark suit the consultant cardiologist was very definitely human after all?

She looked up hesitantly, waiting for the smile of recognition, of remembrance, and felt an ice-cold shock as he frowned, passed the case notes into her numb hands and said abruptly, 'Thank you, Nurse. I'd like to make a brief examination of the patient please, if you'll pull the curtains round.'

Pippa stared at him, eyes wide with shock as he brushed past her to move closer to the bed. There hadn't been as much as a flicker of recognition. She could have been any nurse standing there. The realisation came like a physical blow, blurring her eyes with tears until Sister's voice intruded sharply at her side.

'Thank you, Nurse Benedict. I'll take that. You may go for lunch now and please be back promptly. It's Nurse Roberts's half day and you'll be needed.'

'Yes, Sister.' The words seemed to be forced from her as Pippa handed over the file she had been holding. For a brief instant the dark head rose and she met a frowning gaze before she turned and fled from the ward as quickly as her feet would carry her.

How could she have been such a fool? Her shoes moved soundlessly on the stairs. She didn't see, much less care where she was going. The entire weekend had been, meant, nothing more to him than a brief respite from rigid routine. Her trembling lips were clamped into a line as she fought the urge to burst into tears. She should have known of course. After all, what had she expected? Had she really fooled herself into believing that a man like Julius Sterling would actually fall in love with a very young, very junior nurse?

A swing door opened beneath the pressure of her outflung hand. Yes, she had believed it. It had been real. She hadn't mistaken her own feelings, only his it seemed, and now he was reminding her in the only way possible, the cruellest way, that here, on his own territory, the rules were very different.

She choked on a sob. Had there ever been an emergency call? Or had it simply been an excuse to get away because he had sensed that she was becoming too deeply involved?

She came to a halt, drawing in great gulps of air. Her heart felt as if it had shattered into tiny pieces, but it was one heart Julius Sterling wouldn't want to mend.

'Hey, where's the fire?'

Pippa spun round and Pete Gibson found himself wondering what had happened to cause the stricken look on her pretty face. She stared at him, shaking her head slowly, like someone recovering from a shock, and forced herself to speak.

'Sorry?'

'The fire. I've been chasing you for the last five minutes. Sister sent me for lunch too, but if you're intending to eat, the canteen's the other way—or hadn't you noticed? You look as if the devil himself were after you!'

And that wasn't so far from the truth, she thought bleakly, summoning a smile. 'Sorry, I was miles away.'

'So I gather. How about coming down from the clouds sufficiently long enough to accept an invitation to the pub tonight? We're both off at five. God and Sister Travers willing, of course. How about it?'

Pippa had actually opened her mouth to say no when something held her back. Injured pride? Simply a desire to hit back, to prove that she hadn't been hurt? Whatever it was, she heard herself say yes and forced a smile to her lips as they walked into the cafeteria together to eat a lunch which might have been chaff, for all she tasted of it.

CHAPTER TEN

'YOU'LL LIKE this place. It's nice and cosy but doesn't get overcrowded. Better still, you don't get the entire staff of Clem's looking over your shoulder.'

Which had to be a blessing, Pippa thought, as Pete led her to a corner table in a pub which boasted a very nice log fire, unlit of course, even though the evening air had a distinct chill to it, and which had little in the way of the history its false wooden beams would have liked to proclaim. Still, it was away from the hospital and that was something to be grateful for.

She tucked her bag on the floor beside her and looked round while Pete went to fetch drinks. There was something to be said for dim lighting, too. It made a far better refuge for her thoughts than a hospital ward.

'Here we are then.' Peter placed the glasses on the table. 'G and T with ice and a slice, twice.'

'And very nice.' She sipped the gin and tonic and wondered what Julius did with his evenings, reminding herself forcibly that it was none of her business. But that didn't prevent yet another quick stab of pain at the apparent ease with which he had wiped all trace of their own particular evenings from his mind.

She listened to Pete chattering inanely about work and began to wonder whether he ever thought of anything else, but at least it saved her having to make any more than the minimum of responses, and she threw a smile in his direction every now and again so that he would think she was really interested.

Her fingers strayed to tuck a strand of hair behind her ear, a nervous little gesture of which she was unaware until he looked at her, one eyebrow raised, and said, 'You've not been listening to a word I've said, have you?'

'Yes, of course I have,' she protested defensively. 'I heard every word you said.'

His expression told her he wasn't impressed. 'If you're really bored, perhaps you'd rather I took you home. I realise I'm probably not very good company, but it does take me a while to unwind. It's a fault you acquire after a while, taking the problems of the job home with you. A bad one, I admit, but one of the hazards of nursing.'

Pippa had the grace to feel guilty. After all, it wasn't fair to inflict her own misery on anyone else, least of all a date. She managed a smile. 'I really don't know what you mean. Of course I'm enjoying myself. It's a lovely pub. It's just that I have a bit of unwinding to do myself.'

He smiled dryly. 'They also do very good food. I just asked if you fancied a chicken and chips and you said, "Oh, really?"'

'Oh dear.' She bit her lip, 'Sorry about that. I'm afraid it looks as if I'm the one who's being a bore. Perhaps you should have asked someone else out.'

'If I'd wanted to do that I wouldn't have asked you,' he said levelly, finishing his drink and putting the glass on the table. 'As for being a bore, well you're definitely not that, my sweet. And even if you were, I'd forgive you.'

She felt his arm suddenly move along the bench behind her and draw her closer. Her fingers tightened around her own glass as if it offered some kind of protection. Not that she needed it of course, not from Pete. Just from her own thoughts. She eased herself very slightly along the bench under the pretext of putting her glass down and picked up one of the bar menus which were liberally scattered around.

'I suppose it is difficult to leave work behind, but then it's that sort of job, isn't it?'

He frowned. 'It depends if you're that sort of person. Nursing used to be a vocation. I'm not saying it still isn't, for a lot of people, but you get some who regard it purely as a job.'

Not someone like Julius Sterling, Pippa imagined, and pushed the thought away crossly. She wasn't going to think about him; not now, not ever. 'Well I don't mind admitting, PTS came as quite a shock.'

'It does to everyone, I think.'

'Really?' Her eyes widened as she looked at him directly. 'I thought perhaps it was just me. I got the distinct impression I was the worst student Clem's has ever had—and I'm definitely not going to survive my first year, let alone the full course.'

He laughed, very close to her ear—but then it *was* getting rather noisy as the obvious regulars began to drift in. 'Don't take everything Sister Tutor says as the literal truth. That's just her way.'

'Is it? Well frankly, it's very persuasive.'

'You'll realise as you get further on in your training.'

Suddenly Pippa wasn't at all sure she wanted to

get further on. 'Perhaps I'm not cut out for it after all.'

'Rubbish. That's beginner's nerves, that's all. You should relax a bit. Enjoy yourself. Live for today, that's my motto.'

And tomorrow will be just as miserable, she thought, sighing heavily, as long as there is Julius. She reached for her drink, gulping it in an effort to rid her throat of its sudden constriction. It would have been better if she had never gone to Cornwall. But that was ridiculous. Might as well say she should never have started her training as a nurse. Julius Sterling was a fact of life, an unpalatable one maybe, but he wasn't going to go away just because she made a fool of herself, more was the pity.

Something was nibbling, irritatingly, at her ear. Without thinking she slapped it away, and Pete swore.

Pippa blinked, not knowing whether to laugh or be cross as he sat nursing a reddening cheek. 'Sorry, I wasn't thinking.'

'Obviously not.' He retreated suddenly to a safe distance. 'I'm beginning to think perhaps this was a mistake after all. Wherever your mind is, Benedict, it certainly isn't with me, and I can't say I find it particularly flattering.' He got to his feet and she followed suit instinctively, full of remorse and tears which seemed in some odd way not to be connected with him at all.

'I really am sorry. I just . . . reacted.'

'Well thanks a lot. I don't know quite how to take that, but thanks for the warning. I'm only glad I hadn't got around to anything else.'

The fact that he had obviously intended to made her feel foolish for not having foreseen what would probably have happened. The Pete Gibsons of this world didn't waste their time and money buying gin and tonics without expecting something in return, which was a pity, because he was probably quite nice under different circumstances. The trouble was, being kissed by Julius Sterling seemed to have soured Pippa for any other experience. She fumbled blindly for her bag. Perhaps she was destined to spend the rest of her life as an old maid, slapping the faces of hungry ear-eaters.

'Why don't you stay and have your chicken and chips?' She was edging her way out of the seat, battling against a tide of tears.

'Hell, look, I'm sorry. I didn't mean . . .'

'No, I know.' She had to duck round him to retrieve her gloves. 'It's not your fault. I'm just tired, that's all, and my head aches.' It was true. She couldn't wait to get out into the fresh air, the darkness where she could cry in peace and privacy. 'I'm sorry I've messed up your evening.'

'Forget it.' He made an attempt at graciousness. 'I'll drive you back.'

'No, really. The walk will do me good. I think I'll have an early night.'

He watched as she headed for the door, a tiny figure with a huge pair of eyes in a stricken face, and felt vaguely cheated and disappointed. 'It rather looks as if I'll be having an early evening myself.' He stuck his hands in his pockets, remembered his empty glass and made his way to the bar to restore his sagging confidence. It was a new experience, having a girl walk out on Pete Gibson.

Pippa stood in the street breathing deeply for a few seconds before turning back towards the hospital. It occurred to her that it was going to be quite a walk and perhaps she had been foolish to refuse the lift, but under the circumstances she could hardly go back now and say she had changed her mind.

Digging her hands resolutely in her pockets, she started walking. So much for little out-of-the-way pubs, and there probably wouldn't be a bus for hours. Not that she was in a hurry, anyway. It didn't even matter just at this precise moment if she never saw Clem's again. No, that wasn't strictly true. It wasn't Clem's she was afraid of.

Pippa closed her eyes, then found herself leaping back, dropping her bag in the road as a car suddenly screeched to a halt in front of her. She knew she was shivering as the driver got out and came towards her, but it wasn't the fact that she had almost walked under his car that was the cause of her state of shock. It was the sight of Julius's face staring down at her in tight-lipped anger before he gathered up her bag, gripped her arm and marched her swiftly round to the passenger seat.

'You crazy little idiot. Do you realise you were practically under my wheels? Do you make a habit of walking around with your eyes closed?'

She was in the car without even knowing quite how it happened, and he was climbing in beside her and starting the engine. Panic welled up, and with it an urge to cry, because he was the very last person she had expected to see. But Pippa had no intention of letting him see the effect he was having. She bit her lip hard, surreptitiously wiping a tear from her cheek.

'I'm sorry. I didn't see you.'

'That was pretty obvious,' he said grimly, his eyes briefly leaving the road to look in her direction. He seemed about to say something, then compressed his lips angrily and drove on in silence for several minutes. It gave her time to compose herself, something not made easy by the mere fact of his nearness, and her nose prickled painfully as the tears threatened again.

'Where are we going?'

'Back to the hospital. At least, I take it that's where you were heading?'

She nodded. 'I could have walked quite easily.'

'You could quite as easily got yourself killed. I don't think you had any idea where you were going. I'd been waving at you for the past thirty seconds.'

'I was thinking.' She turned away to stare out of the window.

He studied her profile. 'Obviously nothing pleasant, and why round here for heaven's sake? It's miles from anywhere. Too far to be out alone, especially when it's getting dark.'

'As a matter of fact I wasn't alone.' She wished she hadn't said it as the muscles in his jaw tightened, then reminded herself that it was none of his business anyway who she went out with. There was no commitment, after all. He had been the one to make that perfectly clear.

She reached for a handkerchief and blew her nose.

'Do I take it you've had a row with the boyfriend?'

'No, of course not. Not exactly.'

He reached into his pocket and held out his own crisply laundered hanky without actually looking at her. 'I dare say it's not as serious as you think. Certainly not serious enough to warrant throwing yourself under the first available car.'

'Pete isn't my boyfriend,' she shot at him defensively, and raised only the merest narrowing of his eyebrows in response. If only he knew, she thought, sitting hunched miserably as far away from him as possible. Well at least it proved her right in thinking that the weekend had meant nothing to him.

Mercifully Julius gave no sign of having heard the soft gasp of pain that broke from her before she stifled it with the handkerchief, breathing in the familiar waft of aftershave. She thrust it into her pocket, knotted her hands together in her lap, and stared through the windscreen.

'It was nice to meet your sister. She and Garrard seem very happy.'

'Yes, they do, don't they?' What was he trying to do? Rub salt in the wounds?

'The twins are lovely.'

'Mm.' Her voice came very slowly unstuck. How could he?

'It must be nice for you to be able to go down there. Do you often get the chance?'

She gritted her teeth. 'Not as often as I'd like, especially now that I'm doing my training.'

'That's a pity.'

'Yes, I love Cornwall, don't you?'

His hand tightened on the wheel as he moved into the centre lane. 'Very much. I always have.'

'Oh, you know it well then?'

'Not as well as I'd like to.' He turned to look at her, but she couldn't read the expression in his face in the half-light. 'To be honest, I've never had the time or the inclination for holidays until now. Something I must remedy I think, after a most enjoyable weekend.'

'Oh.' She sat in stunned silence, feeling her heart beat erratically. She couldn't bring herself to say anything as they turned into the drive heading up to the nurses' home. Julius switched off the engine and she was left with the infuriating thought that she would never actually know what he had meant.

In the close, dark confines of the car she was again made acutely aware of the disturbing effect he had—would always continue to have, she re-alised now, no matter how hard she fought against it. And fight she must, as a cruel memory of the moments in his arms hit her like a destructive force until she had to bite her lips to prevent herself from groaning aloud.

She shut her eyes tight, despising her own weak-ness which still made her want him, then began fumbling jerkily for her bag where it had fallen under the seat. He reached it first and handed it to her, but made no attempt to release it. Instead, as her hands closed round it, he drew her closer and kissed her gently on the mouth.

Pippa shivered with the sheer sweetness of it; then he drew away, releasing her abruptly, leaving her feeling as if she was hanging from the edge of a cliff.

'Don't worry, Pippa, these things have a way of working themselves out. They always do. Lovers' tiffs are no great disaster, you'll see. He'll be trying to phone you by the time you get inside.'

She stared at him, disbelieving, as the words came like a slap in the face. But he didn't even seem to notice as he leaned across to open the door. His face was stony, expressionless, as he watched her climb out, and she stood shivering on the steps.

'He'll come round, unless he's a complete fool—and I'm sure he's not.'

'But I've already told you, Pete isn't my boy-friend,' she began crossly, only to clamp her lips together as the car moved away. She stood watching it for some seconds until it disappeared from sight. So much for any interpretation she might have cared to put on his comment about the weekend. It had meant so much that his one concern was to throw her into the arms of the first man who came along. The pity of it was that *he* was the first, and no arms would ever offer that kind of feeling again.

CHAPTER ELEVEN

BY MID-WEEK the headache seemed to have become a permanent fixture and, to top it all, Pippa had a cold as well.

'You look a sight for sore eyes.' Liz fastened the belt round her waist and checked her cap before they both headed across to the main block.

'Thanks a lot.' Pippa sneezed again and made her way up to Men's Surgical with the vain hope that perhaps Sister Travers might by some miracle have decided to take a day off, or, by an even greater miracle, wouldn't notice her.

It became obvious from the minute she entered the ward that neither was on the list of possibilities. There was also a full operating list and second lunch became an order rather than an option.

'I need my senior staff here.' Caroline Travers dismissed the pale face and red eyes as the obvious result of a late night and felt no sympathy. 'You can start by stripping the beds of all the up patients, Nurse, and do the rest as patients go to Theatre.'

'Yes, Sister.' Pippa waited hopefully for some indication of assistance, but it wasn't forthcoming.

'Well, Nurse, get on with it. What are you waiting for?'

'Er, nothing, Sister.'

Caroline Travers disappeared into her office as Pippa dragged the large laundry skip from bed to bed, trying to shut out the dull thumping of her head as she removed soiled sheets and replaced them with fresh ones. Pete Gibson walked past, but she deliberately ignored the pained look he threw in her direction. The strategy worked until she had finished the beds and wheeled the skip into the linen room where he followed her, quietly closing the door.

'I knew I'd catch up with you sooner or later, but you didn't have to make it quite so difficult.'

'I didn't know I had,' she lied. 'I've been rushed off my feet—and anyway, you know what Sister's like. She's watching me like a hawk.'

'Not right now she isn't.'

'Maybe not, but it's just a matter of time.' Pippa looked at the door, wishing he would go away and leave her alone, but he stood watching the varying expressions flickering over the pretty face and told himself that her reactions the previous night had simply been the result of shyness. He'd obviously have to play it more carefully in future.

'Sorry about the other night.' He smiled disarmingly. 'I guess I got a little carried away, but that's the effect you seem to have on me.'

She looked at him steadily, irritated to find herself so easily able to read his mind, and bent to the task of tipping the soiled linen into black plastic sacks. 'That's all right. It was my fault anyway. I expect it was this wretched cold coming on. I should keep away if I were you. I'm probably infectious.' She sneezed effectively into a hanky and was relieved to see him abandon the idea of closing in. She felt quite grateful for the red eyes and nose and far too weary to get involved.

'I was going to suggest we might give it another try some time.'

Pippa gave the notion all of fifteen seconds'

consideration and dismissed it. 'No, I don't think so. Thanks all the same.' She felt genuinely sorry for the look of hurt disbelief on his face until she realised it would last only for as long as it took to make his next conquest. 'Nothing personal. It's just that I'm really going to have to put all my energies into getting through my training.' She offered as a tiny sop to his temporarily bruised ego, 'So I wouldn't be very good company.'

'Oh, I don't know.'

She hid a smile, concentrating on the list she was making as she counted sheets. 'By the way, who's that new girl on Men's Med? She wasn't in PTS so she must have come in from outside. I think she's a third-year. Stephanie something-or-other. You must have seen her.'

'Can't say I have.' He felt, peevishly, that somehow the conversation was slipping out of his control.

'Oh, you must have. She's gorgeous, blonde hair, green eyes. Just getting over a broken engagement, according to the grapevine. Not that you can believe all they say, of course. I gather she was asking about you at coffee the other morning.'

'Really?' A gleam of interest surfaced and was quickly stifled. 'I expect it was something routine. X-rays gone to the wrong ward, something like that. You know how it happens.'

'Don't I just,' she murmured sympathetically, and began the list again for the third time. 'I expect you're right.'

'Still, it won't do any harm to check. Being new I expect she needs someone to show her the ropes, get her used to our way of doing things.'

'I'm sure she'd appreciate all the help she can

get,' Pippa murmured, stifling a chuckle as he muttered something and backed towards the door.

'Well, sorry you feel you have to . . .'

She nodded, sneezed again and waved him out.

At lunch she swallowed two aspirins with her coffee, made a half-hearted attempt at the steak and kidney pie, and finally gave it up as a bad job. She got back to the ward to find herself summoned to Sister's office and tapped at the door trying to list in her mind any sins she may unknowingly have committed and which had suddenly come home to roost.

A voice bade her enter and she did so, to stand before the desk feeling oddly like a prisoner on trial. *And what has the prisoner to say in her own defence?* Her mouth jerked into a smile as the thought rushed into her head. *I can only plead insanity, your lordship.* She managed to stifle a giggle beneath a cough as Sister looked up.

'Did you say something, Nurse?'

'Er . . . no, Sister. That is, you sent for me, Sister.' She felt curiously light-headed. Perhaps it had been a mistake, taking those tablets on a near-empty stomach.

'So I did, Nurse.' Caroline Travers rose to stab a finger at the list on the notice-board behind her. Pippa leaned forward to peer in its direction, wondering whether she was supposed to decipher the minute, spider-like scrawl.

'You will discover a copy on the notice-board outside.' Sister sighed heavily. 'I would suggest that you study it and you will see that you have been put down for a long weekend off next week. It wouldn't normally happen quite so soon, especially as you only recently had one.' Her tone implied that it might normally be several years. 'Unfortunately we are short of senior staff to cover at weekends, so I must make the best use of those I have. You will finish at midday on Friday and be back on duty on Monday morning. Is that quite clear?'

'Yes, Sister. Thank you, Sister.'

'Go along then.' A hand gave imperious dismissal. 'And, Nurse, kindly remove some of that blusher from your cheeks. You know the rules allow nothing more than a discreet hint of make-up.'

'But, Sister . . .' Pippa's hand went to her cheeks, a protest dying on her lips as the dark head was bent purposefully over the papers on the desk. She didn't wear blusher. In fact she didn't wear make-up at all, apart from a delicate hint of lipstick. Was it her fault if she had a high colour?

She stormed to the cloakroom and stared with horror at her face in the mirror. How could Sister not have recognised a temperature when she saw it? The cold must be worse than she had imagined.

She splashed her cheeks with cold water and stood for a few minutes with her eyes closed. Roll on the weekend. She would shut herself in her room, go to bed, and die quietly. With a bit of luck if it was flu she might not even have to go on duty on Monday morning.

The phone was ringing in the lobby of the nurses' home as she came off duty a couple of days later. Since everyone else had gone their various ways, either on duty or joining the rush for the bathroom, Pippa answered it with her mind half on whether she could face sausages for tea or whether just to go without altogether.

'Nurses' home.'

'Hello, Pippa?'

To her amazement she heard her brother-in-law's voice and a surge of pure homesickness brought a ridiculous flood of tears to her eyes. 'It's Garrard. What a bit of luck you answering the phone! I thought I'd have to wait hours for someone to find you.'

She blew her nose hard, revelling in the familiar comfort of a friendly voice. 'Yes, I know it's you.'

There was a muffled crackling and a silence at the other end. 'I say, are you all right? You sound a bit odd.'

'Do I?' She sniffed and laughed. 'Yes, I'm fine. I've got a bit of a cold, that's all.' Cold feet more like, at the thought of bumping into Julius again. 'I think it must have been all that exhilarating fresh air of yours. It went straight to my head.'

She heard him laugh. 'It's strong stuff.'

'How's Emma and the twins?'

'Much better. The twins have the constitution of a pair of oxen. Emma's fine too. She sends her love.'

'Give her mine too.'

'Well, actually,' he hesitated, 'I was rather hoping you might be able to do that yourself. Look, I know it's short notice, but I don't suppose by any chance you've sorted out your weekends yet, have you?'

Pippa frowned. 'Yes, as a matter of fact Sister made the list out a couple of days ago. Apparently I get the honour of being off this coming weekend. Why?'

'Oh, that's marvellous! Look, you'll have to say

if it's inconvenient. I know what you nurses are with your boyfriends and so on.' She choked quietly on a response. 'But the thing is, I've been called away suddenly to speak at a conference over the weekend. The chap who was to have done it is ill or something. Anyway, I've been asked to take over and I was wondering how you'd feel about coming to keep Emma and the infants company? I know she'd like the chance to see you properly now that the twins are feeling a bit more sociable. Oh, and David's tooth is through as well, so he's in a better frame of mind.'

Pippa gulped tearfully. How could he possibly have known that it was what she wanted more than anything else in the world right now?

'I'd love to come. I'm off duty at midday on Friday so I could catch the first train and be there by tea-time.'

'That's smashing. I'll get Emma to pick you up at the station. You're a brick.'

Not a brick, she thought. I'm a fool to think I can escape so easily from the possibility of bumping into Julius every time I turn a corner. Not that he had been in evidence at all since that night, but then he was probably avoiding her.

'You're absolutely sure you're all right? You sound sort of tearful.'

She laughed. 'Honestly, Garrard, you sound like a fussy old hen. I'm fine. Couldn't be better.'

'Oh well, as long as we didn't put you off last weekend. I know things were a bit strained.'

But not in the way he meant. She smiled hollowly at the phone. 'It was lovely, and I'm longing to see you again. Look, I'll have to go. I'm supposed to be at a lecture in an hour's time.'

He rang off and she made her way up to her room, deciding that perhaps she could face something to eat after all.

CHAPTER TWELVE

It was amazing how even a few days could make such a difference, Pippa thought, huddling deeper into her coat, glad that she had decided to give the beach a miss. The trees were showing the first faint signs of autumn, turning to gold and beginning to fall, making a soft carpet beneath her feet as she walked up the lane. Even the sea looked colder and less inviting. Or was it that she was seeing it all through different eyes?

It was just starting to rain. She turned her face up to the drops and thought of Julius's arms round her, lifting her, his mouth kissing her in a way that had seemed to promise so much. She couldn't bear to think of never knowing those sensations again, of having only the one brief memory for the rest of her life. It was a future empty of everything, and one she didn't want.

She paused for a few minutes to watch the business of harvesting going on in one of the fields. The yearly miracle—planting, growing, gathering. Pretty much like the hospital, really. Patients came in, were cured, most of them, and went home again. It seemed odd that right now she couldn't relate her own life to any part of it, and a whole weekend hadn't done anything to lessen the feeling of being adrift. In fact, if anything, it had done the reverse. She had been a fool to come. It was too much like probing a raw wound. Damn Julius Sterling. Her mouth ached with tension as she turned and walked resolutely back towards the house, knowing that nothing was going to be solved by a few days of escape.

Her brain was too confused. How could she possibly have got all the signals wrong? And yet she had. Oh yes, she had quite clearly totally misread the whole situation, and she was the one who was going to have to pay the price in unhappiness for the mistake.

The warm smell of baking cakes met her as she walked into the kitchen, discarding her coat and perching on a stool to nibble at currants. She was glad to have the cold wind to blame for the white misery of her face which she had caught, reflected briefly, in the hall mirror. Was that really herself, that stricken creature with the shadows under her eyes?

She accepted a cup of coffee, wrapping her hands round it as if she would never be warm again, and listened to Emma chattering happily.

'What have you done with the twins?'

'Oh, they're playing quite happily together. It's uncanny, but they seem to have this marvellous method of communication, almost as if each knows what the other is thinking. Don't ask me how they do it, but it certainly seems to work.'

Pippa smiled. Children were lucky. They accepted everything at face value. It was a pity they had to grow up and learn to be hurt.

'What time do you have to get back?' Emma asked.

Pippa looked at her watch. 'There's a train about four. It will get me in reasonably early. I want to get things ready for tomorrow.' The question is, how do I get myself ready? she thought, and drank the coffee, scarcely feeling it scald her throat. If only she wasn't feeling so ridiculously weepy. 'I suppose I ought to go and sort my things out.'

'Are you sure you're all right?' Emma paused in the task of spooning mixture into a sponge tin and licked her finger, a habit never lost since childhood. 'I remember training was pretty deadly. I was always exhausted, but you look absolutely washed out.'

'It's just a cold on top of worrying about the exams, I expect. I was never much good at the written stuff.'

'You were always better than I was. When I think of some of the things I did, I'm surprised any of the patients survived.' Her eyes misted reflectively. 'Some of them were lovely. I remember Sam Hackett, whose wife always insisted on bringing him grapes which he loathed. I was always digging them out of his locker.'

'Things haven't changed much. I don't suppose they ever will.' Pippa leaned her chin on her hands, dipping her own finger into the cake mixture, then sighed as she got down from the stool. 'It's no good. If I don't make a move soon I'm going to miss that train.'

'I do wish you didn't have to go.' Emma gave her an uneasy glance. 'I feel we still have so much to talk about. Are you sure everything's all right?'

'Mm. Fine.' Pippa smiled with enforced brightness, relieved when Emma had to rescue a batch of cakes from the oven.

'How's Julius, by the way?'

She felt her stomach muscles contract. 'Who?'

'Julius, you idiot. Julius Sterling.'

'Oh. I've no idea, but then he is a consultant, you

know. Our paths don't exactly cross too often.'

'Funny. He didn't seem to me the type who'd let a thing like that bother him. Not that I know much about him, of course.'

'I doubt if anyone does. He's a loner and prefers to keep it that way. Which suits me fine.' She felt herself blush as Emma stared at her.

'You sound as if you don't like him, but I thought you two were getting on so well.'

Pippa shrugged. 'As I said, I really don't know him at all, and in any case you can hardly count a weekend, can you? It's a bit like ships passing in the night, holiday romances and all that. They're never quite real somehow, are they?' She turned and made for the door before she made a complete fool of herself. 'I'll finish packing. Are you sure you don't mind running me to the station? I can always get a taxi.'

'You'll do no such thing.' A male voice intruded cheerfully as Garrard came into the kitchen, divesting himself of coat and briefcase. He looked tired but pleased with himself, and Emma launched herself into his arms with a cry of delight.

'Garrard! why didn't you ring? I haven't started any food. I wasn't expecting you for hours.'

'I know.' He stared ruefully at the dusting of flour which seemed to have attached itself to his suit. 'But it all went very well and we finished early, so we thought rather than hang about trying to phone, we might just as well get away before we were cornered. You know what people are like after these conferences.'

Emma stared at her flour-covered hands as if not quite sure how it had come there. 'We? You said *we* got away.'

'Yes, it was a smashing stroke of luck. I had company and got myself a lift back at the same time. Frankly, I wasn't particularly looking forward to the train journey back.' He turned to grin at the figure who walked through the door, depositing a small case on the floor, and Pippa felt her heart give a sickening lurch. 'Julius, come on in. He was at the conference. We met up on the first evening in the bar.'

That explained why she hadn't seen him around.

'Hello, Pippa.'

She felt her gaze drawn unwillingly to the unsmiling face and thought how tired he looked as their eyes met and held for a moment. She had to fight back an urge to go to him, brush the hair from his eyes.

'Hello . . . sir.'

Some expression which might have been anger flickered across his features, but he said nothing. He sat instead on the stool she had just vacated, with Garrard opposite, and drank coffee.

'What's all this about catching a train? You're not going yet, are you?' Garrard helped himself to a hot cake from the cooling rack. 'I haven't had a chance to see you yet.'

'I know. I'm sorry.' Pippa managed to instil some feeling into the words, conscious all the time that Julius was watching her, making her feel oddly uncomfortable. 'But I have to get back. I'm on duty first thing tomorrow and you know what it's like. There are things to get ready and I could do with an early night.'

'Couldn't we all?' Garrard yawned. 'It's a bit silly you going all that way on the train though, when

Julius is going back anyway. Don't you agree, Julius?'

'Absolutely.' The response was calm and told her absolutely nothing about whether he was pleased or annoyed to find himself suddenly landed with a passenger.

'That's very nice of you, but I really couldn't put you to all that trouble.' She heard the note of panic in her own voice and looked directly at the consultant. He got to his feet, apparently unaware or unmoved by the look she flung at him.

'It really wouldn't be any trouble. I have my car and, as Garrard says, it would be quite ridiculous for us both to travel separately. I shall be quite happy to give you a lift.'

'But I . . .' She looked desperately for some excuse. 'I still have to pack. It will take ages and I'm sure you won't want to hang around.'

Again there was the slight movement of the muscle in his jaw. 'That's all right. I'm in no great hurry, as long as we leave within the next couple of hours. I'm sure you can manage to pack in that time.'

Pippa would almost have sworn there was a hint of amusement behind the words, but was in no mood to find out as she threw him a glance of unreasoned hostility before starting up to her room, where it took all of five minutes to pack her jeans, spare sweater, nightie and a toothbrush in a small bag.

Out of sheer perverseness she decided to take a shower, lingering just long enough to let the water trickle over her face and body, cooling its feverishness. She felt utterly weary, but not so weary that she didn't dress quickly and flick a comb through her hair, because it occurred to her that Julius Sterling probably wasn't a man who took kindly to being kept waiting.

Which made it all the more galling when she strolled casually into the kitchen to find him still sitting there, quite unconcernedly helping himself to jam sponge cake, and to be greeted by his casual, 'That was quick. I thought you'd be hours. Most women are.'

And no doubt he was an expert on women, she thought, as he bundled the small bag into the car boot with a distinct gleam in his eye, and saw her settled comfortably in the passenger seat before climbing in beside her.

She sat rigidly, refusing to look at him as they made their goodbyes and finally reached the traffic. She glared silently out of the window telling herself, 'I don't like this man. I hate him. I don't care if I never see him again.'

It was very depressing to discover that not only was it not true, she didn't want to believe it either.

She must have slept. She wasn't sure for how long, but when she woke it was almost dark and she had to blink hard in an attempt to remember where she was. Her arms and legs ached, so did her head, and she felt incredibly unwell. Probably the result of not having eaten, she told herself, detaching herself with as much dignity as possible from the comfort of Julius's shoulder, where her head must have slipped as she dozed.

He looked down at her. 'You needed that, didn't you? Haven't you been getting your proper sleep?'

'Yes, of course I have,' Pippa snapped. 'Cars

always have this effect on me—when I'm a passenger, that is. I'm used to driving myself.'

'In that case it's just as well you weren't driving today. You're not yourself at all, are you?'

She wondered crossly how he could possibly know what her proper self was, but felt too tired to argue or even to notice that he had left the motorway until she saw the lights looming up ahead. She sat up. 'Where are we going? Shouldn't you keep straight on?'

'I probably should.' He was concentrating on the road. 'But I think we could both do with a cup of coffee and maybe something to eat. This service station is pretty handy. I often stop here.' He pulled into a car park which seemed remarkably busy, and switched off the engine. She knew she should move but somehow it was too much effort and she sat with her eyes closed until he spoke.

'It looks a bit wet out there. We'd better make a run for it. Can you manage?'

'Yes, of course I can. Why on earth shouldn't I be able to make it?'

'My dear girl . . .'

'I am not your dear girl.' Her mouth was compressed with misery. In the overhead light she saw his mouth twitch. 'I think that is something we can safely discuss at some other time. Right now you look like death warmed up, and I think a hot drink might do you good.'

He was probably right, except that she felt too ill and miserable to care. 'I'm going to be sick.'

With a quick movement he was out of the car and round to her side, supporting her as she stumbled out and holding her against him until the feeling of nausea passed. Only vaguely did she realise that her head was pressed gently against the warmth of his jacket and that it was a very nice feeling, until waves of humiliation and misery came crashing in and she struggled to detach herself, wondering what on earth he must be thinking.

'I'm s . . . sorry. I really don't know what's happening. There's absolutely no reason. I'm never car sick. I'm a good traveller.' She shivered and at once felt herself drawn closer until his hands cupped her face and he looked down at her.

'Poor Pippa.' He kissed her face so gently that she wasn't sure whether she had imagined it, until he did it again, brushing his fingers lightly against her wet cheek. 'I suppose you do realise you have measles?'

She reacted as if she had been stung, leaping from his arms, her hands clasped to her face in horror. 'It's not true! You're joking, and I don't think it's funny.'

He was infuriatingly calm. 'My darling girl, if you don't believe me, find a mirror. Your face is covered with spots. No wonder you've been feeling so rotten. I'm only surprised we didn't suspect before.'

It was too much. A tear trickled down her cheek to be followed by another and another, until he wiped them away. 'But it can't be measles! I was sure I'd had it.'

'Obviously not. I'm afraid you're going to feel rough for several days, but once the spots are all out you'll start to feel better. Come on.'

'Where are we going?'

'I think we'll skip that coffee after all and just get you to the hospital.' She was back in the car, feeling strangely relieved to be off her legs, which had suddenly developed jelly-like tendencies. 'When we get to the nurses' home you'll go straight to bed with a couple of aspirins and a warm drink.'

She had neither the energy nor the inclination to argue. 'I'm sorry I've caused you so much trouble. I seem to be making a habit of spoiling your weekends.'

He dragged his gaze from the road. 'Whatever gave you that idea?'

She thought, without saying, that it seemed pretty obvious, but closed her eyes instead, pretending to doze. It worked pretty well too, because when she woke two hours later he was drawing up by the steps of the nurses' home and shaking her gently.

'We're here. Can you manage to get yourself to bed?'

Afraid of the consequences if she said no, Pippa nodded sleepily and then experienced an intense feeling of disappointment as he walked up the steps beside her only to let her go.

'I'm going to go over to the main block to let someone know what's happening. You'll probably want to stay in bed tomorrow. I'll see to it that someone covers for you on the ward.' He turned to kiss her in a way which left her feeling utterly confused and much too tired to question it. In any case, she wasn't at all sure she could cope with the answers right now.

'Are you leaving?' She heard the note of disappointment in her own voice and he looked down at her.

'I have to. It won't be for long, I can promise you that, and I wouldn't be going at all unless it was something very, very important. Until then there's only one thing you need to know.'

She tried hard to smile as he kissed her again and told herself she had only imagined that he had whispered, 'I love you.'

'When will I see you again?'

'Very soon. Then I'll explain everything.'

She wasn't sure what there was to explain and gave up the effort of thinking about it altogether as she finally climbed into bed, abandoning herself to the misery of spots and uncertainty until she fell into a deep and surprisingly dreamless sleep.

CHAPTER THIRTEEN

FOR THE next few days things drifted on above and around her, and she was perfectly content to let them happen. In fact the whole weekend had become something of a vague memory, so that she wasn't even sure which parts had been real, which imagination. The only thing she knew for certain as she lay staring out of the window at the rain, was that it had left her feeling depressed and very weak.

A vase of roses strategically placed on the bedside table caught her eye and she smiled. Everyone had been very nice. Far too nice in fact, she thought after the last visitor had gone, leaving her to sleep again. It was all she seemed to have done for the last couple of days. Sleep, drink copious glasses of squash and lie thinking about Julius.

She had even dared to hope he would come to see her. Each time the door had opened her heart had leapt, only to subside into bitter disappointment until common sense told her that when he had said he would see her soon, he had simply meant when she returned to the ward. She was still telling herself she didn't mind when Liz bounced in, still wearing uniform, having obviously just come off duty.

She perched on the edge of the bed, reaching for a grape, and stared enviously at the roses. 'Wow, aren't they gorgeous? Lucky you. Who sent them?'

'I've no idea. I woke this morning and they were there. One of the staff brought them across from the main block, I expect. They always seem to have more than they know what to do with.'

Liz looked slightly doubtful. 'Mm. They look rather special. Still, one of the perks of being an invalid, I suppose. Better make the most of it.'

'The *only* perk so far as I can see,' Pippa grumbled, sitting up to reach for her dressing-gown. 'I haven't exactly enjoyed myself lying here, you know. I had no idea measles could make you feel so ill.'

'It's probably your age.'

'Oh, thanks a bunch.'

'No, I'm serious. They always say these things are worse if you get them as an adult rather than as a child.'

'Yes, well they're right.' She forced her arm into a sleeve, frowning at the feeling of lethargy which still seemed to remain. 'I was so sure I'd had it though.'

'It must have been the other kind.' Liz stared at her own face in the mirror. 'Come to think of it, have I?' She suddenly seemed less happy. 'I thought I had a spot this morning. You don't suppose . . .'

'No, I don't.' Pippa shuffled out of bed to the window. 'You're far too healthy. The only thing you'll have is stomach-ache if you keep on eating those grapes. Not that I mind in the least, but there was a good-sized bunch there when you came in.'

A few offending stalks littered the empty plate. 'Oh dear. Sorry. Still, pity to let them go off.'

'Not much chance of that. How's everything been in my absence, anyway?'

'Oh, ticking over much as usual. I'm sorry to

have to tell you this, but the hospital has managed to carry on. Seriously though, everyone missed you and sends their love. Apparently Travers is furious. She clearly thinks you arranged it on purpose, just to spite her.'

'She would. As if anyone would choose to go through this.'

'I wouldn't mind a few days in bed. Not having to get up and on duty would suit me down to the ground. Nothing to think about all day.'

If only that were true. 'Frankly, you're welcome to it.'

Liz put her feet up on the bed. 'When are you back on duty?'

'In a couple of days, all being well. The spots have almost gone. I feel a bit of a fraud, actually, lying here.'

'I don't see why. You were quite ill. I know one thing, if I have children they'll all have their injections. I couldn't face a row of spotty faces all staring at me over the bedclothes.'

'You know your trouble? You've got no heart,' Pippa protested.

'I know.' Liz grinned. 'Anyway, I suppose I'd better go if I'm going to get any lunch. I'll pop in again tonight if you like.'

'I'll be glad of the company. Not that people haven't kept popping in, but it's nice to have a real natter. I've missed being on the ward. I didn't think I would; isn't it silly?'

'Well, if it's any consolation at least you won't have to put up with Mr Sterling the minute you come back.'

Pippa felt her heart give an uncomfortable lurch. 'Why, what do you mean?'

'Just that he hasn't been around for a few days and the fact has been noted, you might say.'

Pippa lay back again quickly. 'Do you know why he hasn't been around?'

'Probably on leave. Sunning himself somewhere, I shouldn't wonder. Lucky devil. I wish he'd asked me along, I'd have gone like a shot. Not that a man like that is likely to be short of females falling over themselves to share his sun-tan oil, I shouldn't think.'

'I expect you're right.' Pippa summoned a smile which didn't match her feelings. It was ridiculous, coming to terms with the fact that she cared desperately. That she missed him to the point where a mental vision of him smiling at another woman became a physical pain. She shivered and Liz looked at her with a measure of concern.

'Are you sure you're ready to go back on duty? You still look a bit peaky.'

'I'm fine. Too much lazing around, that's the trouble. I need some exercise.'

In fact she wasn't quite so sure she hadn't been just a little hasty as she dressed later, standing on legs which still felt remarkably wobbly. And the sight of her face in the mirror as she brushed her hair had added an even greater shock. The spots had disappeared but her eyes looked like dark smudges in the whiteness of her face. Appalled, she resorted to a defiant touch of make-up, adding a trace of lipstick to her mouth before venturing over to the cafeteria.

One thing was certain. She had to get back to work, and the sooner the better. The alternative was to sit around thinking, and right now her thoughts made far too depressing companions.

Sister took one look at her face, however, and immediately squashed any idea of having her back on the ward. She closed the office door promptly, as if to cut off the escape route of any lingering germs, and retreated to sit at the far side of her desk.

'I'm sorry, Nurse, I can't imagine how you thought you could possibly go back on to a ward looking like that.'

Having spent half an hour applying what she had thought was a very good screen of make-up, Pippa heard the words and felt a ridiculous urge to weep. 'But, Sister, I'm much better. My spots are gone, so I'm not infectious, and I'd really much rather be back at work.'

'Very commendable, Nurse, I'm sure,' Sister retorted. 'We could certainly do with an extra pair of hands, but frankly you would be very little use to me as you are. I understood you were told to take at least another three days off.'

'Yes, Sister.' Pippa muttered the words under her breath. Another three days, and no sign of Julius.

'Then in that case I expect you to take the doctor's advice. Why else do you think it was given?' Sister dropped a file into her drawer and closed it sharply. 'A nurse who is likely to faint on the ward is a danger not only to herself but to the patients. Why do you think we make these rules, Nurse? Certainly it isn't for our convenience. Just take yourself off and find something to do—some quiet reading or pastime. Haven't you any studying to catch up on?'

'Yes, Sister.'

She was dismissed and retreated bleakly from the

office, wondering how on earth she was going to fill the extra days without going slowly mad. Where was Julius? Why hadn't she heard? They were the thoughts which went over and over in her mind as she tried to concentrate on an essay. But it was no use. She couldn't concentrate, her head ached. Even walking didn't help, not when she found herself looking at every figure who turned a corner and knew a crashing disappointment when it wasn't Julius.

The truth must be, she finally acknowledged it, that he didn't care. It had all been words, or perhaps sympathy. She got up from the chair, threw her book aside and reached for her coat. In the telephone booth she started dialling the number, cut the connection, closed her eyes, then started again. She was being weak, she was doing all the things she had said she would never do, but she had to find some answers, whatever they were.

Garrard's voice answered. 'Pippa, you're better. We've been worried sick, blaming ourselves.'

'Really, there was no need. I'm fine.'

'Well, you can imagine how we felt when Julius rang to give us the news. We couldn't believe it. Mind you, Emma said she knew something was wrong. She just didn't imagine it could be measles, of all things.'

Pippa leaned weakly against the window of the box. 'Julius told you?'

'Oh yes. He rang the night you got back. Frankly he sounded awful. Come to think of it, I hope he isn't going in for it too. My God, what have we done?'

For a second the idea was almost welcome. 'No, I'm sure he's fine. I heard he's away on holiday, probably sunning himself somewhere. I expect he must have told you about it.'

'Oh.' Garrard was obviously thinking about it. 'He may have done. Actually I think he did say something . . . about France, I think. It was only in passing. I gather he goes there quite often. Lucky devil. I hadn't realised he was taking a holiday though. Still, I don't blame him. I expect he can do with it. I thought he'd been looking pretty tense lately. Perhaps when you see him you'll pass on our love.'

'Yes, I'll do that. Give mine to Emma and the babies, won't you?'

'Will do. Do you want to speak to Emma? She's upstairs with the twins, quelling a minor rebellion.'

'No, that's okay. Don't bother her now. I'll ring again. Thanks again though for putting up with me.' They went through the niceties. Pippa wasn't even really aware of what they said, and she rang off feeling weepy and even more depressed. Obviously it hadn't been such a good idea after all. The only thing it had told her was that Julius had a life of his own and that she didn't form any part of it. None of which prevented her from thinking about where he was, what he was doing and, in particular, who he was doing it with.

CHAPTER FOURTEEN

IT CAME AS something of a shock to hear Sister telling her she was to be moved.

'I'm sorry, Nurse. It's nice to see you back, but I'm afraid we've had to do some reorganising while you were away, so I'm sending you over to Women's Medical. If you'd like to go straight over there, Sister Philips is expecting you.' Lisa Carson smiled at the dejected face in front of her. 'It's not so bad, you know. I always quite enjoyed the medical wards.'

'Yes, Sister.'

'Off you go then, and best of luck. I'm sure we shall see you back here fairly soon.'

Walking across to Women's Med, Pippa felt herself curiously detached from everything. The only consolation was that Liz was there to greet her, grinning from ear to ear as she honed in, one eye surreptitiously on Sister, the instant her friend walked through the door.

'Great. I heard first thing you were being sent over. You'd better go and report to Philips. She's in the office. Then, with a bit of luck, we'll have a chance to natter later. I'm down for first coffee so I'll look for you then.'

'Fine. I think I'm going to need it.' Pippa made her way to the office where she tapped at the door and was beckoned in by a tall, attractive figure.

'Ah, you must be Nurse Benedict.'

'Yes, Sister.'

'I hear you've just had measles. Poor you. Spots all gone?'

'Oh yes, Sister.'

'Jolly good. Well, I'll get someone to show you the ropes.' She beckoned through the window and a third-year nurse came in.

'Yes, Sister?'

'This is Nurse Benedict, just over from Surgical. Show her what goes where, will you? There's nothing to worry about,' she smiled at Pippa. 'The routine is pretty much the same on every ward. You'll soon get the hang of it.' She peered at her watch. 'I think you'd better take first coffee. It will be easier until you know what's what. Doctors' round is at nine-thirty, so we'd better all get a move on.'

They were banished with a cheerful wave and Pippa found herself in the ward beside Julie Weston who proceeded, pleasantly, to put her in the picture. She was a nice girl, tiny, dark-haired, clearly popular with both patients and staff as was demonstrated when one small figure beckoned timidly from one of the beds.

'This is Mrs Timson, in for tests and feeling very nervous. Hello, Mrs Timson. How are you feeling this morning?'

'Not too good, Nurse. I didn't sleep very well. Couldn't seem to settle somehow. It must be the strange bed.' The elderly face seemed to be strained, searching for something. Pippa smiled, hoping it hid her own nervousness, glad to leave it to the other girl to do the necessary reassuring.

'Now you're not worrying about the tests are you, Mrs Timson?'

'Well I don't know what's going to happen, you

see, and when will they let me go home? I can't stay
too long. There's no one to look after Stan.'

'Stan?'

'My husband. He's useless when it comes to
looking after himself.'

'Well he's going to have to learn, just for a little
while, anyway. Haven't you any family who'd give
a hand?'

'I suppose so.' The reply came defensively. 'But
it's not the same, is it? And he won't like it.'

Julie smiled patiently. 'No—well it won't be for
long, and the tests are really nothing to worry
about. You'll be having another blood test later
today. You've had one before so you know what
happens, don't you? Then I expect Doctor will
want an ECG, but it won't hurt, I promise. All that
happens is that we take a sort of reading of the way
your heart is working. It tells us an awful lot and
Doctor will be able to decide whether perhaps you
need medication to steady things down a little.'

They spent several more minutes at the bedside,
and when they finally left, Mrs Timson was looking
decidedly happier and was even tucking into her
breakfast.

'She had a very slight heart attack,' Julie explained. 'She seems to be making a good recovery,
but one of the major problems is getting over to her
that she's no longer thirty years old and can't be
expected to be as active now as she was then. You'd
be surprised how difficult that is at times, especially
with women. Some of them take it almost as a
personal insult, but you just have to take time to
explain. In fact it's quite a big part of the job,
whatever they are in for.'

As they walked down the ward Julie filled in

details about as many of the patients as she could. 'We have twenty-six in here, varying ages and conditions. Mrs May is in for tests and will probably be transferred to Women's Surgical tomorrow for an op. Mrs Jeffries had a suspected ulcer. Seems to be responding nicely to medication. You won't take all this in at once, but you'll soon get to know them all.'

Pippa wasn't so sure. 'I was only just beginning to recognise the faces on Men's Surgical. It's a bit confusing to be moved so soon.'

'Yes, I know. I heard about the measles. What rotten luck. A bit tough on the love-life too, I should think. Not exactly romantic, is it?'

Pippa managed a laugh as they whisked along the ward. 'Not exactly.'

'Look, would you like to tidy those lockers? Mr Jones will be doing his round this morning. He's the registrar. Usually it will be Mr Sterling, but he's still away. In France I hear, and very nice too. Of course, you may not know him. He's the cardiologist. Quite a dish—everyone likes him. Most of the staff secretly call him the Bachelor of Hearts, but I suspect a few illusions are about to be shattered where he's concerned.'

Pippa felt suddenly quite cold and her fingers jarred clumsily against a glass of water, spilling a little on to the locker. 'How do you mean?'

Julie came round the bed, whisking magazines out of sight. 'Well, only that he's due back in a few days and there have been vague murmurings that he's bringing a Mrs Sterling with him. Talk about a dark horse. You wouldn't think he could keep a secret like that, would you? Especially not in a place like this.'

Unless of course it hadn't been secret because it had only just happened. Pippa had to clamp her teeth over her lip to prevent it quivering. She had to turn away rather than let the girl see how the unthinking words had affected her. It couldn't be true, not after the things he had said. And yet why not? Her brain offered the bleak response. It would explain so many things. His going away, the fact that he had said he couldn't tell her why. 'I . . . I suppose it's not so surprising really, is it?' Her voice wavered faintly, but Julie didn't seem to notice.

'I wonder what she's like?'

'I wonder.' Pippa heard herself whisper it even while in her own mind she was already sure she knew exactly what the new Mrs Sterling would be like—the sort of person Julius would fall in love with.

'Well, we'll find out soon enough, so there's no point in speculating.'

Pippa's head jerked up. 'Why, what do you mean?'

'Oh yes, I forgot. You don't know, do you? Only that he's bringing her in as soon as they arrive from France.'

'You mean . . . here?' Pippa felt suddenly very cold. 'But why?'

'No idea,' Julie shrugged. 'All we've been told up to now is that she'll be in for observation, something to do with her heart.'

Compassion and shock mingled, draining the blood from Pippa's face. Oh no, not that. No matter what her own feelings were, she couldn't bear it if he was to lose the one woman he had chosen to love. Surely fate couldn't be so cruel . . .

She had to walk away. She felt incapable of

speech, of anything except acute misery which seemed to fill every corner of her being. It was all so horribly cruel, so unfair, and worst of all was the fact that his wife would be coming here, to this very ward.

'Go to coffee now, Nurse.' Sister's voice brought her back to reality and Pippa muttered something in response, meeting up with Liz so that they ran down the stairs together. But she didn't go for coffee. Instead she made some excuse, pleading a headache, and rushed away to the cloakroom, telling herself that there she could break down in peace and privacy. But it wasn't that easy. She stood waiting for the tears which wouldn't come. Perhaps it was too soon yet. She still had to come to terms with the fact that he was married . . .

'You okay?'

She jumped as Liz poked her head round the door. 'What? Oh yes, fine.' She blew her nose hard and washed her hands, splashing cold water on to her face.

'Well Sister's on the rampage. I thought I'd better warn you.' Liz came to lean against the wash-basin. 'You're sure there's nothing wrong? Only you've been looking a bit odd all morning.'

'Yes, honestly.' Pippa pushed her hanky into her pocket and straightened her dress. 'Liz, do you know anything about Mrs Sterling? I mean . . . what she's like?'

'Haven't a clue. But I'm intrigued, I can tell you that, along with ninety-nine per cent of the hospital population. It seems no one had a clue, and you wouldn't think a thing like that could be kept quiet, would you? Not in a place like this. Mind you, I'm not really surprised. A man with his looks would have to be snapped up pretty quickly, more's the pity.' She sighed. 'Not that I ever stood a chance, worse luck. I'm strictly not his type.'

'I wonder who is?' Pippa whispered shakily. It was like rubbing salt into the wound, but she had to ask. 'You don't know . . . Well, how long?'

'No idea. But one of the junior housemen was saying that Sterling pops over to France quite often. He obviously had good reason. Just think, a honeymoon on the French Riviera . . .' She stretched languidly. 'I'd settle for that, wouldn't you?'

Pippa murmured something. Her voice came out hollow and unreal, but then there was nothing real about any of it. Why couldn't he have told her? Why had he had to go and kiss her? Let her believe a thousand things that had never had a single chance of ever coming true anywhere except in her own mind and dreams?

'I've been such a fool.' She wasn't even aware she had whispered the words aloud until Liz gave her an odd little look as she re-applied a touch of colour to her lips.

'Did you say something?'

'What? Oh, no. Just telling myself I'm a fool. I should have asked for a week of my leave.' Then she could have been miles away when he came back to Clem's.

CHAPTER FIFTEEN

THE DAYS passed in a round of numbing similarity. Under any other circumstances, Pippa supposed, she would have enjoyed Women's Med. The patients were, on the whole, very eager to get well and go home, and, in the main, that was precisely what happened. Pippa found herself responding to their needs with a warm cheerfulness which had been forced at first, until she discovered that in a way, while not exactly shutting out her own feelings, as long as she was on the ward she could keep a firm barrier around them. It was only at the end of the day that it seemed to crumble and needed to be painstakingly rebuilt before anyone could glimpse what was behind it. It worked well too, until about a week later.

All the routine admissions had come in the previous day and were settling in nicely. Visitors had just gone, leaving behind the usual mass of flowers which she was arranging quietly in the kitchen when Sister poked her head round the door.

'Nurse, leave that for now. You're needed on the ward. Quickly please, we have an admission coming in.'

Pippa followed the hurrying figure, wondering what they were to prepare for. 'Is it an emergency, Sister?'

'No.' Sister flapped her hand in the direction of a plastic linen sack which was hastily removed. 'But Mr Sterling phoned to say he's on his way in with

Mrs Sterling. We've been expecting her for some time, of course, but it was a matter of arranging transport. I gather she's been having some sort of treatment in France.' Sister frowned, unaware that Pippa had frozen briefly to a halt behind her.

So this was it then. Over the past days she had tried to steel herself for it. In her more cowardly moments she had even prayed she would be off duty.

'We're going to have to put her in the small side room. I'm afraid we're full in here. Go and check that everything's ready please, Nurse, then go down to Records and tell them they haven't sent up the file I asked for on Mrs Sterling. It's bound to be the first thing he asks for.'

Pippa did as she was told, checking the room, which was partitioned off from the rest of the ward and often used for sudden admissions or patients who were particularly ill and needed a greater degree of privacy and quiet. Her actions were automatic as she moved about the room, mechanically noting that the clipboard was in place, with its new sheet awaiting the first details of the patient. She drew back the curtains, folded back covers and found herself wondering about the woman who would shortly be occupying the bed. She walked quickly back to the ward, knowing that she couldn't bear to face the moment of arrival, the sight of Julius's face, strained with tension . . . and love.

Staff Nurse Cross bustled back from her tea-break, and Pippa stood quietly awaiting Sister's permission to go down to Records as Staff was put in the picture.

'Mrs Sterling is being brought in now by ambulance.' Sister scanned the brief notes which had just been handed to her. 'I understand she has a history of heart trouble and is coming in for a thorough check up, but Mr Sterling is accompanying her so we shall get more details when he arrives. Is the bed ready, Nurse?'

'Yes, Sister.'

'Fine, then go and fetch the records please, and be as quick as you can.'

Pippa fled, her feet skimming down the stairs, telling herself that it was just another patient, that she was a nurse, or hoped to be some day, and that personalities were something she must learn to accept without becoming involved. But it was too late. She *was* involved. This woman had intruded uninvited into her life, and she resented it bitterly.

All right, so I'm a coward. She pushed the thought aside. She couldn't simply stop loving him just because that love wasn't returned. If only she could shut out the memories, find some magical formula to ease the pain.

She reached Reception only vaguely aware of the ambulance drawn up outside and the figures coming towards her. They were all seen through a mist of tears and it wasn't until one of them came to a halt in front of her that Pippa dragged her gaze up to see Julius smiling at her. The slight pressure of his hand on her arm was enough to set her pulse racing and it struck her that he probably didn't even know he was being cruel.

'Pippa, I have to talk to you.'

She snatched her hand away suddenly, needing fresh air. 'I'm sorry. I'm on duty. I have to go.' She caught his look of shock and didn't care.

'It won't take a minute. There's something I must explain.'

She didn't want explanations. All she wanted was to be alone. 'Just leave me alone! What can there possibly be to say?' Through a haze of tears she prayed he would find an answer, waited as he tried to say something.

'Oh, Mr Sterling,' Sister caught him with a look of relief and shot a glance at Pippa's white face. 'Mrs Sterling is being taken up to Women's Medical now. Her notes are all ready and she is asking for you.'

A nerve pulsed in his jaw. 'I'll be right there, Sister.' He seemed angry. 'Pippa, when can I see you?'

She swallowed hard and turned away. 'Please, leave me alone. You don't need to say anything, just go to your wife, she's waiting for you.'

She ignored his outstretched hand, heard him call out after her as she ran, but she didn't turn back. The sight of him standing there might have broken down her carefully built defences.

By the time Records had managed to unearth the file and she had returned to the ward, there was no sign of him, and her heart thudded with miserable relief. She wasn't going to be able to avoid him for ever, but right now was what counted. A breathing space. Time to adjust, if that would ever be possible.

For the rest of the morning she managed to keep out of the way, glad to be kept busy. She found herself purposely avoiding the small side room, wondering what the occupant was like, yet not really wanting to know. She would be pretty of course; young, frail and very much in love.

She stopped short as Sister came towards her. 'Nurse Benedict, take these flowers into Mrs

Sterling's room please. Aren't they beautiful?'

Pippa stared at the bright red roses and flinched. 'I'm supposed to wash Mrs Crawford's hair, Sister.'

'That's all right, Nurse. I'm sure she won't mind waiting five minutes more. Here you are. Find a vase and arrange them nicely.'

Sister walked away leaving her clutching the blooms, and as she arranged them her heart ached as if each deep red flower was a kiss or memory returned, something to which she had had no right.

Her hand froze as she hesitated outside the door, then her chin rose. After all, all she had to do was go in, smile as if it were any other patient, arrange the flowers and leave. With sudden resolution she pushed the door open and stopped short as she found herself staring at the occupant of the bed. A pair of bright eyes viewed her from a face framed by silver-grey hair. Pippa came to a halt. She must have come to the wrong room, or the patient had been moved. There had to be some mistake. She had expected to see a young woman. This one must be sixty-five, and while decked out in a pretty pink bed-jacket and delicately laced nightie, was certainly no frail beauty.

'But, I don't understand.' Somehow she forced her frozen limbs into action. 'Mrs . . . Mrs Sterling? But I thought . . . '

The room's occupant chuckled. 'No more do I, my dear. It's all a great deal of nonsense. I was never in less need of a check-up. As if I were an old lady, which I am not.' The twinkling eyes took in the roses and the shaking hands which held them. 'Since middle age is now considered to be nearer fifty, I reserve the right not to consider myself old until I reach ninety.' She arranged the covers neatly, removing a pile of magazines to the locker beside a very large box of chocolates. 'I'm afraid this must be very inconvenient for you all, having me thrust upon you like this. I did try to tell Julius it was all quite unnecessary, but he does fuss so.'

Pippa stood, roses in hand, doing her best to gather her reeling senses. 'J . . . Julius?' She swallowed hard, not quite knowing whether to laugh or cry.

'Are those for me? How like him to send roses. Whatever else I may say about my son, he is always thoughtful. He knows that particular shade are my favourites.' She took the blooms, breathing in the heady perfume. 'Not that I'm fooled for one minute of course. He thinks a little bribery will make me change my mind, and it won't. I'm still very cross.'

She didn't look it, Pippa thought, as the blue eyes twinkled mischievously. 'I'm sorry you're not happy.'

'Oh my dear, take no notice. After all these years I should have learned by now that Julius isn't a person one argues with. He's just like his father.'

Was he? Pippa wondered, telling her heart sternly to stop its erratic thudding. She carried the roses to the locker, rearranging the stems carefully, remembering the ones which had stood at her own bedside not so very long ago. It was strange how everyone seemed to prefer red.

'Would you like me to leave them on here?' She stood the card which bore his large scrawled handwriting against the vase. It was signed 'Love, Julius.' All too easy to do. She sighed heavily.

'That's splendid. Not that I intend staying here long enough to see them wilt. It's all far too silly, insisting I have a check-up just because I had a few twinges years ago. I'm as healthy as any woman of my age has any right to be. I'm afraid my son is a bully.'

Pippa hid a smile. 'I expect he's just concerned for you.'

'Pooh! Well there's absolutely no need. A little excitement never did anyone any harm. Quite the contrary, although I must confess, I was beginning to think Julius would never settle down. He works far too hard. And then, suddenly, just when I'm thoroughly enjoying myself, he tells me, quite matter-of-factly if you please, that he intends getting married and seems surprised when I'm a little taken aback.'

Pippa felt the ground move suddenly beneath her feet. 'G . . . getting married?'

'So I am told, which is why I am here. So that I shan't disgrace myself by becoming over-excited on the day. As if it were likely.' Mrs Sterling put her feet out of bed and reached for a glamorous négligé. 'I assured him I have every intention of meeting this paragon who has managed to turn him into a human being at last, and I have no intention of being put off by a few silly aches and pains. Julius takes it all far too seriously. Whoever she is, she has to be the sort of girl I would admire enormously.'

Pippa leaned faintly against the locker, scarcely caring that it might be Sister who came through the door at that moment, until the voice behind her spoke.

'Now, Mother, and just where do you think you're going? You're supposed to be here to rest.'

'Julius!' The blue eyes sparkled, destroying the validity of the note of annoyance in her voice as her arms were held out. 'I do hope you're not going to start preaching at me. I was resting perfectly well in the sun on the Riviera until you came along and snatched me away. I've been telling Nurse here what an incorrigible bully you are. Why, the poor little thing looks terrified of you herself, and I'm not surprised.'

Pippa wished the ground would open and swallow her up as the shrewd gaze came to rest on her stricken face. He had no right to have the sort of effect he was having upon her heart. 'Is that true, Pippa? Are you terrified of me?'

Mrs Sterling's expression slowly took on a look of curious delight as she looked from one to the other. 'Pippa? Julius, you don't mean to tell me I've been prattling away and all the time . . . Oh, how absolutely delightful!'

'Mother, before you utter another word,' he gave the warning as he rounded on Pippa, 'I think we have something to say to one another.'

Her eyes flung a look of horror in his direction before she began to head for the door. What was there that they could possibly have to say? 'I have to get back to the ward.'

He forestalled her, reaching the door first to bar her way and, to her chagrin, gripped her arm, sending an agonising shiver of delight running through her.

'Please let me go.'

'Certainly. When we've had our little chat, Pippa. Mother, try to behave yourself while I'm gone.' He sighed. 'Why is it that the women in my life always seem to provoke difficulties?'

'My dear Julius, it isn't we who do the provoking. I do believe you are the most obstinate creatures.'

The door closed and Pippa found herself being whisked along the corridor, the firm grip on her arm tightening as she struggled, allowing not even the remotest possibility of escape.

'Where are we going?'

'Just somewhere where we can have our little chat in peace, without fear of interruption.'

She slapped at his fingers crossly. 'I suppose you realise Sister is going to be absolutely furious?'

'Does that worry you more than the fear of annoying me, Pippa?'

She shot him a glance as he flung open the door of the day room, thrust her inside and stood with his back against it, presenting a forbidding warning to anyone who might consider intruding.

'You have no right to be annoyed.' She faced him, breathing hard.

His brow rose fractionally. 'Oh, but I think I have. What was all that nonsense about avoiding me down in Reception when I tried to speak to you?'

'I did not.' She sniffed hard and frowned as he moved dangerously closer.

'But I think you did, Pippa. You scuttled away like a frightened rabbit. And what was that hysterical outburst about my wife?'

She tried to back away, hating him for the effect his nearness could have. 'Well I thought . . .'

'What precisely did you think?'

His aftershave was doing incredible things to her emotions again. 'Well, they all said it was . . . your wife.' She finished feebly, not daring to look at him.

'And you believed it?'

'Well how was I to know?' She thought she heard him chuckle softly, but when her gaze flew up to his, his face was very serious as he looked down at her.

'My dearest, darling Pippa.' Her heart thudded crazily. 'Just what sort of man do you think I am?'

She didn't want to think about it. 'I . . . I don't know.'

The dark brows drew together. 'I find that very hard to believe. I thought I'd made my feelings very clear.'

'N . . . not to me.' She sniffed again, brushing a tear away as he took her in his arms. 'How could I know what you were thinking, especially when you did your very best to throw me into Pete Gibson's arms?'

'I'm sure I didn't quite do that,' he said very quietly.

'But I told you he wasn't my boyfriend and you didn't seem to want to believe me.'

'My darling, I had to be sure. If there was any chance at all that you and he . . .' His mouth was grim.

'There wasn't. It was never like that, but I couldn't convince you, and how was I to know what you were thinking?'

Suddenly he had drawn her much closer. 'My darling Pippa, one thing you can be very sure of; when I kiss her, the woman I love will know exactly what I have in mind. Like this.' He kissed her, a very long, very clever kiss, and she closed her eyes because she felt as if she was drowning. When he let her go she tried to open her eyes and couldn't.

'Open your eyes, Pippa.'

'I can't.'

'Look at me.'

She did and he kissed her again. She sighed and closed her eyes. 'This could go on all night.'

'If you wish,' he said quietly. 'That is and always was up to you, my darling.'

Her lashes flew open and she blushed, furiously.

'And what are you thinking about now?' His finger traced the line of her cheek.

'Your mother is right. You *are* a bully.'

He laughed softly. 'My mother knows me very well—but then, she should. I take after her. I always like to get my own way.'

'Oh, do you indeed?' She tried to pull away. 'And what if I don't choose to let you?'

'Is that what you choose?'

She glared at him, knew it wouldn't work to try and be angry, and subsided weakly. 'No. But I still don't understand what's happening. Just when did you decide . . .'

'That I loved you? My darling girl, from the minute I saw you, even more so that day on the beach. If you only knew how much I wanted to make love to you.'

She stared at him incredulously. 'But you were beastly.'

'It seemed safer, for both of us.'

It was something she didn't choose to argue with as he took her in his arms again, until she remembered with sudden shock that she was supposed to be on the ward and that her cap was all askew and her hair falling out of its pins. Horrified, she pulled away.

'Sister isn't going to like this at all.'

'I could answer that.' His mouth twitched. 'But I won't.' And he drew her back into his arms, where she felt the last of her very weak resistance crumble. 'We're going to be married very soon, aren't we, my darling?'

She didn't answer and he tilted her head back to look at her, frowning. 'Well, say something.'

'I can't. I don't know what to say.'

'Try, "Yes, Julius."'

'Yes, Julius.'

He smiled. 'There you are, that was easy, wasn't it?'

It was, she thought. Far too easy, and snuggled closer in his arms. Sister definitely wasn't going to like this at all. She giggled, then forgot everything as she gave herself up to his kiss. Poor Sister!

A romance of searing passion set amid the barbaric splendour of Richard the Lionheart's Crusade. Intrigue turns to love across the battlefield... a longer historical novel from Mills and Boon, for only £2.25.
Published on 12th of July.

The Rose of Romance

Mills & Boon

4 Doctor Nurse Romances
FREE

Coping with the daily tragedies and ordeals of a busy hospital, and sharing the satisfaction of a difficult job well done, people find themselves unexpectedly drawn together. Mills & Boon Doctor Nurse Romances capture perfectly the excitement, the intrigue and the emotions of modern medicine, that so often lead to overwhelming and blissful love. By becoming a regular reader of Mills & Boon Doctor Nurse Romances you can enjoy SIX superb new titles every two months plus a whole range of special benefits: your very own personal membership card, a free newsletter packed with recipes, competitions, bargain book offers, plus big cash savings.

AND an Introductory FREE GIFT for YOU.
Turn over the page for details.

**Fill in and send this coupon back today
and we'll send you
4 Introductory
Doctor Nurse Romances yours to keep
FREE**

At the same time we will reserve a
subscription to Mills & Boon
Doctor Nurse Romances for you. Every
two months you will receive the latest
6 new titles, delivered direct to your door.
You don't pay extra for delivery. Postage and
packing is always completely Free.
There is no obligation or commitment –
you receive books only for
as long as you want to.

It's easy! Fill in the coupon below and return it to
**MILLS & BOON READER SERVICE, FREEPOST, P.O. BOX 236,
CROYDON, SURREY CR9 9EL.**

Please note: **READERS IN SOUTH AFRICA** write to
Mills & Boon Ltd., Postbag X3010,
Randburg 2125, S. Africa.

- -

FREE BOOKS CERTIFICATE

**To: Mills & Boon Reader Service, FREEPOST, P.O. Box 236,
Croydon, Surrey CR9 9EL.**

Please send me, free and without obligation, four Dr. Nurse Romances, and reserve a Reader
Service Subscription for me. If I decide to subscribe I shall receive, following my free parcel of
books, six new Dr. Nurse Romances every two months for £6.00*, post and packing free. If I
decide not to subscribe, I shall write to you within 10 days. The free books are mine to keep in
any case. I understand that I may cancel my subscription at any time simply by writing to you. I
am over 18 years of age.
Please write in BLOCK CAPITALS.

Name _____

Address _____

_____

_____Postcode_____

SEND NO MONEY — TAKE NO RISKS

Remember, postcodes speed delivery. Offer applies in UK only and is not valid to present subscribers. Mills &
Boon reserve the right to exercise discretion in granting membership. If price changes are
8DN   necessary you will be notified. Offer expires 31st December 1985.
* Subject to possible V.A.T.

EP1